Samuel French Acting Edition

Your Flake or Mine?

by Jack Sharkey

I0591857

SAMUEL FRENCH

SAMUELFRENCH.COM   SAMUELFRENCH.CO.UK

FOR PRODUCTION ENQUIRIES

UNITED STATES AND CANADA
Info@SamuelFrench.com
1-866-598-8449

UNITED KINGDOM AND EUROPE
Plays@SamuelFrench.co.uk
020-7255-4302

Each title is subject to availability from Samuel French, depending upon
country of performance. Please be aware that *YOUR FLAKE OR MINE?*
may not be licensed by Samuel French in your territory. Professional
and amateur producers should contact the nearest Samuel French
office or licensing partner to verify availability.

Please refer to page 102 for further copyright information.

CAST OF CHARACTERS

(in order of appearance)

TONY DAWSON, a writer of greeting-card verse
IRVING MOSS, Tony's best friend, a professional student
CORAL KELLY, chic chanteuse at a Hollywood hotspot
MARGO CORCORAN, a high-toned executive secretary
LUCILLE LARRABEE, Tony's copy editor
SAGAMORE DUNSTAN, a breakfast-food manufacturer

TIME: The Present, midsummer
LOCALE: Tony's office/apartment in L.A. area

ACT ONE: A Friday afternoon
ACT TWO: That night
ACT THREE: About a half-hour later

For my wife

PAT

from her favorite flake

Your Flake or Mine?

ACT I

Curtain rises on the modest apartment of TONY
DAWSON, *somewhere in the Los Angeles area, on a
Friday afternoon in midsummer, so room is cheery
and bright. Starting from downstage left, we see the
rear three-quarters view of a TV console, angled to
face a pair of armchairs — one just above and one
just right of a small, low coffeetable — set slightly
left of and slightly below center stage; farther
upstage of the TV is a cabinet at least a foot taller
than the TV, against the lower left wall; a door in
the wall upstage of this cabinet leads to the apartment hallway, and a door in a wall-section parallel-
ing the upstage wall leads to a walk-in closet just
upstage of the hall door; if both these doors were
opened at once, they would meet edge-to-edge, and
encompass an area just slightly larger than a phone
booth; there is a potted plant in the area; to the
right of the closet's right wall is a dinette area with a
small table and two chairs before a drape-flanked
picture window in the upstage center wall; through
the window can be seen blue sky and nothing else,
since the apartment is on an upper floor; right of
the dinette area is a kitchen area with a range and
refrigerator against the upstage wall just right of the
window; a large folding screen at least six feet tall is
blocking most of our view of this kitchen area; the
screen is a four-section type, with some kind of
Japanese-print panels; these are translucent paper,*

5

*and extend all the way to the floor with no gap
beneath; dinette and kitchen areas are eight inches
higher than the rest of the stage, and this platform
continues downstage about six feet below the
screen, till it reaches a wrought-iron rail, parellel to
the proscenium, which is downstage of a doorway
in the right wall that gives access to the apartment's
bathroom; on the wall between this doorway and
the proscenium hangs a large bulletin board, its sur-
face covered with tacked-on greeting-cards, type-
written sheets of paper, and a few newspaper clip-
pings; there is a large desk with a complementary
swivel chair beside this bulletin board, set so that a
person seated at the desk will be facing directly out
front; a typewriter and telephone are on this desk,
along with various writer's tools — a cannister of
pencils, tray of typing paper, stapler, etc.*

At curtain-rise, TONY DAWSON *is seated at desk, scowling
at a page in the typewriter, and quite motionless,
though his fingers are poised over the typewriter
keys;* TONY *is not unhandsome, and casually dressed,
probably in his early 30's. After a moment or so,
there is a KNOCK at the hall door.*

TONY. (*Without moving from his stance or looking
away from page.*) Come in! (IRVING MOSS *enters, and
manages to get the door closed; this is difficult because
he wears a sweatsuit and sneakers and is jogging, and
continues to jog in place even while pausing to shut
door;* IRV *is about* TONY'S *age, pleasant of face, and
slightly tending toward paunchiness; when the door is
shut, he starts jogging toward platform which gives onto doorway [this area just upstage of railing will*

henceforth be simply referred to as "platform"], speaking en route:)

IRVING. Hey, Tony, can I use your bathroom?

TONY. (*Will maintain paperward stare and finger-poised stance until specified otherwise.*) First give me a rhyme for "silver."

IRVING. (*Will continue jogging till specified, so he now veers from his platformward direction, and will jog down right of armchair area, left below it, up left of it, and right above it, during their dialogue.*) There *are* no rhymes for "silver."

TONY. Come as close as you can.

IRVING. I didn't know you cared.

TONY. To the *rhyme*!

IRVING. How about "pilfer"?

TONY. "*Pilfer*"?!

IRVING. Yeah. You know. Like robbing, looting, stealing—

TONY. Irv, this card is for Mother's Day!

IRVING. So the guy's mother is a shoplifter. (*NOTE: If* IRV *completes his circle of the armchair-area before their dialogue ends, just have him repeat it as often as necessary.*)

TONY. But it's such a lousy rhyme.

IRVING. It's close.

TONY. Not close enough.

IRVING. So don't *say* "silver"—say "*silfer*"!

TONY. Why would the guy pronounce it "silfer"?

IRVING. Maybe his mother is from Heidelburg!

TONY. This card is supposed to sell in America!

IRVING. There must be *some* guy in America whose mother is from Heidelburg!

TONY. Oh, go to the bathroom!

IRVING. (*Gratefully.*) I thought you'd never ask! (*Completes jog to exit toward bathroom.*)

Tony. Oh, the hell with it, I'll make his mother's hair *white*! (*Will strike out word on page, retype new word, during:*) Plenty of rhymes for that. W-h-i-t-e . . . There! (*Sits back, reads from paper in typewriter.*) "As you sit there in your rocker, with your hair becoming white . . . "

Irving. (*Off.*) "Spread some cheese upon a crocker, 'cause it's Mother's Day tonight!"

Tony. (*Winces.*) *Irv*-ing . . . !

Irving. (*Off.*) I was *only* trying to *help* you!

Tony. Yeah, right into the *unemployment* line! (*Abruptly, we hear ALARM CLOCK BELL from within cabinet;* Tony *grimaces, rises, moves to cabinet, opens door, takes out clock, and as he STOPS BELL,* Irv *jogs back in onto platform, shakes head as he watches* Tony *replace clock inside cabinet and close it, then starts jogging doorward upstage of armchair-area on his line:*)

Irving. About *time* you woke up, Tony—it's nearly sundown!

Tony. (*Crossing below armchair-area toward desk.*) That was to remind me to stop *work*!

Irving. (*Jogging in place while opening hall door.*) Now I *know* you're crazy. Most guys need a reminder to *start* work!

Tony. (*Will start neatening desktop items, during:*) I wanted time to straighten up the place before Margo arrives. (*On the name,* Irv *stops jogging instantly.*)

Irving. Margo? *Your* Margo? Coming *here*?

Tony. (*Has set some desktop items into still-open desk drawer.*) She is no longer *my* Margo, and it's *not* a social call. (*Slams drawer shut as "period" to statement and topic.*)

Irving. (*After a moment of staring at* Tony's *back,*

closes door quietly and takes a step toward him.) Then what?

TONY. (*Out front, not wanting to face him.*) Just — some details about the divorce. (*Starts re-neatening already-neatened desktop items.*)

IRVING. (*Quietly concerned, still immobile, just upstage of armchairs.*) I thought that was all wrapped up and over with.

TONY. (*Shakes head with rueful smile, but does not face IRV yet.*) Not in California. We still have to split the community property.

IRVING. (*After an incredulous glance about the room.*) *What* community property? (*Will start moving down toward TONY on:*) The only item of any value is your typewriter. How do you split *that*?

TONY. (*Finally facing him, with resignation.*) It's on-ly a technicality. We'll work it out.

IRVING. She's already got the house and car. What's she after now, your neckties?

TONY. She's not after anything. The house and car were that judge's idea. I just have to sign a paper saying we're both content with the split. (*Takes a bottle from deepdrawer of desk.*) Would you like a drink?

IRVING. Don't you mean *half* a drink?

TONY. I bought this after the divorce. It's all mine.

IRVING. In that case, I'll have a double. (TONY *will cross to cabinet and get two glasses, while* IRV *folds screen to reveal refrigerator and range, and gets a tray of icecubes out of refrigerator, over their dialogue:*)

TONY. What happened to your diet?

IRVING. I only diet on the days I don't jog. It all evens out.

TONY. You can't mean your waistline.

IRVING. I prefer to lose poundage gradually. That way the fat won't come back.

TONY. It never left.

IRVING. I've got that all worked out: This fall I join the track team.

TONY. As what, the mascot? (*By now,* BOTH *are at armchairs—* TONY *at right one,* IRV *at upstage one—and are putting ice and liquor into glasses.*)

IRVING. I need some variety in my education. I'm nearly through with pre-med, there's a waiting-line for engineering, and I'm not much interested in law.

TONY. How many degrees do you have now?

IRVING. Three or four. Who counts? UCLA has hundreds of electives I haven't even used yet.

TONY. Just how long do you think you can keep this marathon *going*? (BOTH *are seated, now, comfortably sipping drinks.*)

IRVING. (*Shrugs.*) How long can they keep the *university* going?

TONY. Don't Grandfather Moss's lawyers ever raise a stink?

IRVING. Sure, but I've got 'em over a barrel. He said in his will that I get twenty thousand dollars a year till I complete my education. Is it *my* fault there's so much to learn?

TONY. You're shameless.

IRVING. I'll drink to that! (*Does so; then:*) Actually, all this education hasn't been a *total* waste of time: I can do the Sunday Times Crossword in fifteen minutes.

TONY. But what about your future—meeting a girl, settling down, having kids?

IRVING. Listen, buddy, I meet *plenty* of girls. Freshmen coeds go for mature men—and I'm almost as old as the professors!

TONY. Okay, so you don't lack for dates. But what

about marriage?

IRVING. (*Piously.*) I'm saving myself till the right girl comes along. (*With sudden unholy glee.*) It could take *years*!

TONY. (*Laughs despite himself; then, a bit more seriously.*) I don't know if I'd recommend waiting for that Girl of Girls . . . that's what *I* did, and you know the result.

IRVING. I thought you never wanted to talk about it again. Back in June, you said—

TONY. The divorce decree was still quivering between my shoulderblades. It's a little easier now.

IRVING. How so?

TONY. (*Thoughtfully, trying to put his emotions into words.*) I didn't know how bad a person *could* feel till Margo left me. So—whatever happens to me from now on could never feel as bad as that. It puts me a little ahead of the game.

IRVING. (*Interpreting sympathetically.*) Life can hold no further terrors?

TONY. You got it, buddy. (*Drains his drink, stands.*) Now maybe you'd better jog on home. I think I can face Margo okay alone—but I don't think I can put up a brave front for two at a time.

IRVING. (*Stands, finishes his own drink.*) Does Margo have any idea how hard the divorce hit you?

TONY. I doubt it. It's the only thing keeps me going—knowing she's happier without me. If only one of us can be happy—I'd rather it was her.

IRVING. Stop, you're going to have me crying all over my sweatsuit!

TONY. It could *use* a washing! (*He will take both empty glasses and start for archway, while* IRV *takes bottle back toward desk, during:*)

IRVING. *Must* you be clever *all* the time?

TONY. (*Shrugs philosophically.*) How else could I write greeting-cards for a living? (*Exits through archway with glasses.*)

IRVING. Some living! A dollar a line! You must have to knock out ten cards a day just to pay the rent on this crummy little apartment!

TONY. (*Off.*) So what *else* have I got to do?

IRVING. (*Leaves bottle atop desk, will return for icecube tray at coffeetable and take it toward refrigerator during:*) But why don't you shift gears and create something more commercial? The monthly magazines pay about a thousand bucks for a short story—and if you ever hit with a *novel*—!

TONY. (*Off.*) What would I *do* with the extra money?

IRVING. You could afford a place with a kitchen sink! (*As he puts icecubes back in refrigerator,* TONY *enters through archway without the glasses.*)

TONY. Cut it out. You're starting to sound like Margo. (*Will go to desk, put bottle back into drawer.*) Economics was *not* our pleasantest topic of conversation.

IRVING. But you were writing greeting-cards when you *got* married.

TONY. She says she thought it was just to pay my way through college. You know, something I could knock out fast between classes and exams.

IRVING. And then came graduation.

TONY. Did it ever!

IRVING. (*Moving toward hall.*) Actually, Tony— from a woman's standpoint—and by that, I mean from an economic standpoint—

TONY. Look, let's drop the topic, or I'll be breaking up with you, too!

IRVING. Does that mean I'd get half your liquor?

TONY. (*Laughs, moving toward him.*) Oh, shut up and get out of here!

IRVING. (*Has hall door open now.*) Sure you don't want me to stick around?

TONY. What for?

IRVING. Moral support. I could distract both of you from weeping.

TONY. Margo doesn't know *how* to weep.

IRVING. You could give her lessons.

TONY. *Irv*-ing—!

IRVING. You cried for two weeks when she left you.

TONY. I'd rather she never found out.

IRVING. (*Shrugs.*) Only trying to help.

TONY. I know.

IRVING. (*Moving into hall.*) Listen—I'll keep an ear open at my apartment, and when I hear her leave—well—I could come back here with a bottle of my own, and—

TONY. (*Touched, but suddenly very weary.*) Keep handing me the Kleenex? . . . You're on! But for now—scram, huh? I have more important things to do than stand here and chat, and so do you!

IRVING. What do *I* have to do that's so important?

TONY. You have to take a shower.

IRVING. (*Sniffs his own general vicinity, then nods.*) You're right. (*Jogs out door on:*) See you later, old buddy!

TONY. (*Calls after him.*) Don't forget to bring that bottle!

IRVING. (*Off.*) And two straws! (TONY *laughs and shuts door, then comes down and stands in angle between armchairs, looking from one to the other, then moves one slightly nearer the other; PHONE RINGS; he crosses to desk and answers it.*)

TONY. Dawson Enterprises, Tony Dawson speaking
. . . (*He suddenly gets a guilty look.*) Oh. Hi, Lucille
. . . The Mother's Day copy—? Uh—(*Lifts corner of sheet
in typewriter, winces as he looks at page, then lies:*) Just
mailed it this morning! (*Drops corner of sheet, looks
guiltier than ever, on:*) Yes, by Monday, I'm sure . . .
What? . . . Oh, yeah, the Christmas stuff, too! (*Lifts
sheet from beside typewriter, shakes head, drops it back
onto desk.*) Yeah, mailed them both in the same
envelope! . . . Yes, I know the new catalogue's coming
out next month. You'll have the stuff, I swear. . . .
Yeah, you have a nice weekend, too . . . Right . . . 'Bye
now! (*Hangs up, looks at papers in typewriter and on
desk.*) I'll be lucky if I have any of this by Valentine's
Day! (*There is a KNOCK at door; he reacts with min-
gled panic and anticipation—smoothing his hair, his shirt,
hurrying toward door, taking knob—then pausing and
taking a deep breath and sighing it out—then he opens
door, and* CORAL KELLY, *a 20-year-old beauty, steps into room.*) Coral! What are *you* doing here?!
    CORAL. Well, when you didn't show up at the club last
night with my new material—
    TONY. (*Slumps.*) Oh, damn.
    CORAL. (*Resigned.*) You forgot *again*!
    TONY. You mean I've forgotten *before*?
    CORAL. Say, you *are* in a bad way! Brother, when you
even forget you *forgot*—!
    TONY. (*Belatedly gestures her toward armchair, shuts
door.*) It's this stupid career of mine. I live like a clam,
seven days a week, can't tell one day from another
unless someone reminds me.
    CORAL. (*Sits demurely in upstage armchair.*) Am I to
understand, then, that you don't even *have* the material
you didn't bring me last night?

TONY. (*Facing her from right of armchair.*) Not exactly—

CORAL. Do you have it or don't you?

TONY. Of course I do! It's—just not down on paper, yet. (*Taps temple.*) Still up here—someplace—

CORAL. But Tony, this is Friday, and I'm supposed to have the new act all memorized and rehearsed by next Tuesday! If I show up tonight *without* it I could lose my *job*!

TONY. I know, I know, and I'm sorry, truly sorry, Coral. Maybe—if I work on a crash-program basis—I could have it in a few hours—

CORAL. (*Sits back, folds her arms.*) Okay, I'll wait. I trust you.

TONY. But you *can't*! I mean—*I* can't work with people in the *room*.

CORAL. (*Stands.*) All right, I'll wait in the hall.

TONY. No, that's *worse*! I mean—look—somebody's coming by, and if she sees *you*—

CORAL. "She"? Oh, Tony! You're not writing nightclub acts for *strangers*?!

TONY. She's *not* a stranger! I mean—she can't act! I mean—

CORAL. (*Turns away.*) Is she—very pretty?

TONY. Gorgeous! But that's not the point!

CORAL. Then what *is* the point? You promised to write a new act for me, and instead you're writing one for her!

TONY. I am *not*! She's not here for writing, she's here for business!

CORAL. (*Faces him, confused.*) But writing *is* your business!

TONY. It's *her* business!

CORAL. Aha!

TONY. I mean, *our* business!

CORAL. Yours and mine?

TONY. Mine and hers!

CORAL. And just *what* line of work is she *in*?

TONY. She's in the breakfast-cereal business.

CORAL. Like your ex-wife was?

TONY. She *is* my ex-wife!

CORAL. Margo?! Coming here? Why?

TONY. (*Tired of the topic.*) I'm all out of cornflakes!

CORAL. (*Hurt, starts for door.*) If you're not willing to *level* with me—

TONY. (*Stops her.*) I am! On the level, Coral! It's just—some paperwork about the divorce, that's all.

CORAL. Then why mustn't she find *me* here?

TONY. Because up to now it's been a *friendly* divorce! I mean—

CORAL. Tony, you told me you and Margo were through!

TONY. We are!

CORAL. So what does it *matter* if she finds me here?

TONY. We'd be even *througher*!

CORAL. (*Surprised, but not angry.*) Tony! You want her back!

TONY. Of *course* I do!

CORAL. Well, why didn't you *say* so! (*Starts for door again.*) I understand perfectly!

TONY. Coral, you're a darling! And I'm sorry about your new act!

CORAL. Oh, relax! I'll just get somebody else to write it.

TONY. By next Tuesday?! Like *who*?

CORAL. (*As* TONY *opens door for her.*) *Joe Shimko* is a fast worker.

TONY. (*Shuts door.*) Joe Shimko?! He only wants to get you up to his apartment!

CORAL. Why shouldn't I go up to Joe Shimko's apartment?

TONY. Because he's a fast worker!

CORAL. Tony! You're jealous!

TONY. Don't be ridiculous! I don't envy Joe Shimko—I just don't trust him!

CORAL. But I need that new material!

TONY. Coral, Joe Shimko couldn't find a rhyme for "moon" in the middle of June! I'll do the material. I swear! Trust me!

CORAL. Are you saying that becouse of *me*, or because I'm paying you five hundred dollars?

TONY. Both!

CORAL. (*Flings her arms about his neck.*) Tony, you *do* care!

TONY. (*Trying to pry loose.*) Not romantically, damn it! (*Manages to grab her upper arms and hold her at arm's length.*) Listen, you are a sweet and lovely young girl—you don't know enough about men—I just don't want you to get hurt!

CORAL. That sure *sounds* like you care!

TONY. I'd care about *any* girl in Joe Shimko's apartment!

CORAL. Really? Then maybe I *ought* to go there!

TONY. Aw, Coral—honestly—you're very attractive—you really are—and if I were free—

CORAL. If? You *are* free!

TONY. Because some stupid *judge* says so? Look, it takes *two* to make a divorce! *Margo* wanted it, *I* didn't. When I said "till death do us part" I meant it!

CORAL. Let me get this straight—Margo's not married to *you* anymore, but you're still married to *her*?

TONY. (*Shrugs helplessly.*) I know how stupid it must sound.

CORAL. (*Softly.*) It's not stupid at all, Tony. It's beautiful. I wonder if your ex-wife knows what a terrific husband she's got!

TONY. (*Takes hold of doorknob.*) Well, she'll never take the time to find *out* if she catches *you* here!

CORAL. (*Nods.*) Gotcha! I'll clear out! (*She turns toward door, and there is a KNOCK at the door, and* BOTH *recoil from it in sudden panic.*)

TONY. It's *her*!

CORAL. What'll we *do*?

TONY. (*Yanks open closet door.*) Quick, into the closet!

CORAL. But what if she's wearing a coat?

TONY. (*Shuts door.*) Okay, then, into the bathroom! (*Grabs her elbow, half-drags her toward platform.*)

CORAL. But what if she has to *use* the bathroom?

TONY. She can't. The half with the door is mine! (*He releases her, and she continues onward, exiting through archway as he turns and lurches back to apartment door, stops, forces himself to be calm, then opens door;* MARGO CORCORAN *enters; she is about his own age, cool and impersonal in a business suit, but nonetheless a knockout, even if her manner is aloof and businesslike.*)

MARGO. Hello, Tony.

TONY. Oh, Maggie, it's so good to see you again!

MARGO. (*Icily.*) The name is "Margo"!

TONY. But I always—

MARGO. That was before the divorce! Let's keep this businesslike, okay?

TONY. (*Defeated.*) Okay. (*Closes door.*) But it *is* good to see you again.

MARGO. Thank you. It's—good to see you, too.

(*Before he can warm to this trace of amiability, she quickly changes the subject.*) So *this* is your new home! Who's your decorator—Erskine Caldwell?

TONY. *I* happen to *like* the place!

MARGO. (*Has moved to desk, glances down at page in typewriter.*) I'm glad *one* of us does. Still hot at it, I see. (*Reads aloud.*) "As you sit there in your rocker, with your hair becoming white . . . " What's this one, a Clairol commercial?

TONY. That's the start of a Mother's Day card!

MARGO. (*Turns to face him.*) "Grandmother's Day" is more like it! I mean—honestly—white hair in a rocking chair?

TONY. (*Brightens.*) Hey, that's a neat rhyme! Thanks!

MARGO. (*Abruptly angry.*) There! You're doing it again! You never stop, do you!

TONY. What are you talking about?

MARGO. Everything's a greeting card! Our entire married life, I don't think we exchanged five sentences without you coming up with a neat rhyme!

TONY. (*Inadvertently doing that very thing.*) I didn't rhyme all the time! (*Winces, chagrined.*)

MARGO. Aha!

TONY. That was an accident!

MARGO. Oh, no, not with you! It's an instinct—a built-in rhythm-machine in your brain! You can't control it—and I can't live with it!

TONY. Aw, honey, don't! If I promise I won't—(*She just folds her arms and stares at him in silent triumph; he realizes, and valiantly tries again.*) Now, look here, my writing career—(*Stops, a bit frightened, tries again.*) There must be a way that I can say—(*Stops, horrified.*) Ye gods! I *do* do it, don't I!

MARGO. (*Nods, no longer triumphant.*) Even on our wedding night.

TONY. I didn't!

MARGO. Oh, *didn't* you! (*Turns downstage, envisioning the moment with weary gloom.*) There I was, in my loveliest nightie, feeling warm and secure in your arms, our lips just inches apart — and do you know what you said?

TONY. (*Shrugs.*) Not — not word for word, of course — but it must have been something romantic —

MARGO. Oh, it was! I'll grant you that, all right!

TONY. Well, exactly what *did* I say?

MARGO. (*Quoting grimly, still out front:*) "Kiss me, darling. Hold me tight. I'm the happiest man in the world tonight!"

TONY. Well, I *was*!

MARGO. (*Faces him.*) But did you have to *rhyme* it?!

TONY. You didn't complain *then*! Hell, come to think of it — you rhymed right *back* at me!

MARGO. (*Takes a backstep.*) I never!

TONY. Oh, *didn't* you! The words were no sooner out of my mouth when you clutched me even tighter, and said, "Tony, honey, don't talk funny!"

MARGO. (*Turns away.*) That was an accident!

TONY. Well, so was mine!

MARGO. (*Moves toward armchair area.*) No. Not yours. It's ingrained. You're never without it, this "rare gift" for lyricizing! The greeting-card business found a real treasure when it latched onto *you*!

TONY. (*Moves after her as she sits in upstage armchair.*) There you go, belittling my work again! I happen to be very proud of what I do!

MARGO. You never did have a head for business.

TONY. (*Sits on upstage arm of right armchair facing her.*) There's more to life than making a buck!

MARGO. Listen, kiddo, it's a rough world outside your cozy cocoon. Ideals are fine and dandy, but they don't put the mashed potatoes on the table!

TONY. You never ate a potato in your life. Now, if you'd said mineral oil and watercress—!

MARGO. Tony. Let's not start in on each other. This is going to be painful enough even if we do it calmly.

TONY. *Must* we do it calmly? You're talking about two shattered lives. I'd much rather we raged and screamed about it. That'd be the *human* approach, Maggie—

MARGO. I *hate* that name, and you know it!

TONY. You do not. You just hate *me*, and you're taking it out on my terminology!

MARGO. I do *not* hate you! (*She winces, not having meant to say that, and he brightens.*)

TONY. Then why did you divorce me?

MARGO. (*Floundering.*) That—that has nothing to do with my feelings for you—!

TONY. (*Stands.*) *What*?! Maggie—are you saying—you mean—you still *love* me—?!

MARGO. (*Miserably.*) Of *course* I do! I just can't stand *living* with you!

TONY. But, if you love somebody—

MARGO. (*Comes to her feet.*) Look, I also love kangaroos and chimpanzees, but I draw the line at sharing my *bed* with them!

TONY. (*Reaches for her.*) Aw, honey—!

MARGO. (*Pulls away, moves toward desk area.*) Tony, cut it out! We have business to discuss and I don't care to do it during a wrestling match! (*Has come face to face with bulletin board, reacts.*) What the hell is this?

TONY. (*Moving to join her.*) What?

MARGO. (*Reads from paper on board.*) "Greetings,

furry little stranger, looking like a collegiate Lone Ranger."

TONY. That's a specialty card. In case someone gets a pet raccoon.

MARGO. (*Turns to face him.*) I'll bet *that* one's a best seller!

TONY. They can't *all* be gems!

MARGO. (*Takes his hands.*) Oh, Tony—Tony—don't you see?! That's the whole problem! The *only* problem! I keep trying to be practical about life, and you keep typing out lousy little verses that nobody will ever buy—!

TONY. (*Reverses grip so that he now holds her hands.*) Maggie, listen to me! The world is filled with unhappy people, people who don't know how to communicate, tongue-tied little people who *need* somebody like me to put their feelings into *words* for them! So maybe I'll never get rich at it—is that so damned important?

MARGO. It is when the *rent* comes due!

TONY. Did we ever miss a payment?

MARGO. (*Pulls her hands free, faces downstage.*) That's not the point!

TONY. Then what *is*? If you love me, and I love you, and the rent gets paid every month—

MARGO. (*Faces him, raging.*) *It's not enough*!

TONY. What's that supposed to mean? Every marriage has its ups and downs. Were you seriously hoping for nothing but ups?

MARGO. (*Pushes past him, moves toward armchair area.*) I don't know what I was hoping for, Tony. I just know—I didn't find it. So—can't we handle this in a civilized manner?

TONY. *You* better handle it. You're civilized enough for the *two* of us.

MARGO. (*Turns to face him.*) Was that a crack?

TONY. (*Approaches her, contrite.*) Aw, Maggie—I'm sorry—Margo—I didn't mean it. You know I'd never do anything to hurt you. But—when you say "civilized"—all it means to me is "coldblooded and ruthless." And you're not like that.

MARGO. There! That's exactly the sort of blindness that led to our breakup. You obviously don't know me at all. Tony, I *am* that way—icy, self-controlled, ambitious, hardheaded—you name it! And you—you're a dreamer, Tony. We were fools to think we could live our lives together.

TONY. There was nothing cold about you on our honeymoon.

MARGO. (*Avoids his gaze.*) Oh, stop it! Please. Stop it. It's over, all over. Face up to it, Tony. I have.

TONY. Hey—are those *tears* I see in your eyes—?

MARGO. (*Wipes angrily at her eyes.*) It's just the damned L.A. smog!

TONY. There hasn't been a smidgion of smog for two days.

MARGO. And how would *you* know? You never leave your little microcosm! Type-type-type, day and night—I'm surprised you know what *day* it is! (*Flashes him a narrow-eyed speculative look.*) What day *is* it, Tony?

TONY. Uh—

MARGO. (*Sighs.*) That's what I thought.

TONY. Friday! (*She looks at him.*) And the month is July! (*A little less confidently.*) Or—early August at the lastest. (*When she simply looks at him, he slumps.*) Oh, hell. You're right. I never *was* much on calendar-watching. (*Gestures her to upstage armchair, moves toward right armchair.*) Sit down, and let's get our business over with.

MARGO. (*Will sit in armchair, but speak with less self-assuredness.*) Yes. Let's. Tony—about our divorce— I've—I've come to a decision—

TONY. (*Sits in right armchair, watching her curiously.*) Then why do you sound so indecisive?

MARGO. (*Avoiding his gaze.*) It—it settled things a bit too fast. About the house and car, I mean. But—I've been thinking it over, and—well—Tony, I want *you* to have them.

TONY. Won't that judge who awarded you everything but my lungs be upset?

MARGO. Look, he gave them to me—I'm giving them to you. Simple as that.

TONY. But honey—!

MARGO. Look, the house and car are yours. Enjoy!

TONY. Is that what's on those papers?

MARGO. What papers?

TONY. The ones I'm supposed to sign, remember? That's why you're over here.

MARGO. (*Stands.*) Oh, Tony, Tony, you're such an innocent! Don't you know that a final divorce decree *is* final?! There's no more paperwork. It's all over, done with, finished.

TONY. (*Stands.*) But when you phoned me, you said—

MARGO. That was just an excuse to come over here, so I could tell you—tell you that—that I—

TONY. (*Reaches for her.*) What are you trying to say?

MARGO. Lay one finger on me and I'll scream so loud there'll be a SWAT team breaking down your door!

TONY. (*Pulls his hands back from her.*) I was only—

MARGO. (*Contrite.*) Oh, look—I don't mind you touching me—(*He reaches again, but retracts his hands again, on:*) But *don't*! It distracts me. And—I've got to tell you—oh, Tony—listen—it's a big ugly world we live in—people aren't as nice as you imagine—even me—Tony, I—oh, damn it, don't you even wonder *why* I'm giving you back those things? Hasn't it crossed your mind to be curious about where *I'm* going to live if I give you the house? (*When he just stares at her, she braces herself, then says:*) Tony, I'm getting married.

TONY. (*Drops back to seat on arm of chair, stunned.*) You're kidding! Aw, Maggie, tell me you're kidding! It's agonizing enough being without you—but thinking of you married to someone else—!

MARGO. (*Angrily, to keep from crying.*) And what did you *think* I was going to do? Sit around staring at our wedding pictures? Of *course* I'm getting married! And I intend to be the happiest bride in the history of wedlock! No doubts, no memories, and no regrets!

TONY. (*After a long, shocked silence.*) Who—who's the guy? Do I know him? When did you meet him? When did you have *time* to meet him? Settling down with a stranger—!

MARGO. Tony, I've known this man for years!

TONY. You mean—even when you and I were married—you and he were—?

MARGO. (*Instantly apologetic and concerned.*) Oh, wait, I can't have you thinking *that!* There was *nothing* between us—nothing *romantic*, anyhow—not until the divorce! But then—(*He stands, almost speaks, but she forestalls him.*) No, please hear me out! After the divorce—that's when he finally declared himself, told me how he'd felt about me all along, and—well—

TONY. You were lonely, hurt, needed someone—

MARGO. Oh, look, I don't feel like parading my emotions, Tony. Let's just say that that's when I realized I liked him, too, and—

TONY. Do you love him?

MARGO. Tony, that's really none of your business!

(*Turns, starts toward door.*) Just accept the fact that there's a new man in my life, now, and—and—(*Near door, turns to face him, unhappily.*) Try to think kindly of me, okay?

TONY. Kindly? Of you? (*Moves upstage to her during his speech.*) How else have I *ever* thought of you? Much as it breaks my heart to say it—if this guy can make you happy—then I guess I can't give you an argument—(*Has reached her, takes her hands.*) Your happiness is all I ever wanted, Maggie.

MARGO. (*Too upset to react to the name, lets him continue holding her hands, but turns her face away from him, miserably.*) Tony, don't. Please don't. Get mad—rage—scream—stop being so damned understanding! It wasn't an easy decision—don't make it harder!

TONY. (*Abruptly drops her hands, moves deskward.*) I need a drink!

MARGO. (*Very churned up inside.*) If you don't mind—I'll have one, too. (*When he pauses en route to give her a hopeful look.*) A *small* one!

TONY. (*Starts for desk again.*) It's *only* eighty proof, Mrs. Dawson—oh, excuse me—Miss Corcoran! (*Will get bottle out of drawer during:*) By the way, just who *is* this long-time lover who's held back so very nobly from declaring himself until your husband was safely out of the way?

MARGO. You don't have to be sarcastic!

TONY. (*Moving to cabinet for glasses.*) Oh, that's right, we're being civilized, aren't we!

MARGO. (*Warningly.*) Tony—!

TONY. (*Will get two glasses, move back to desk and pour two short drinks from bottle, during their dialogue.*) Okay, I'll cool it. But who *is* the lucky guy—? And he's luckier than any man has a right to be!

MARGO. (*After a pause.*) Sagamore.

TONY. (*Reacts.*) Your *boss*?!

MARGO. (*Wryly.*) How many Sagamores *are* there?

TONY. (*Moves to her with the two drinks.*) But—you can't mean it—*Sagamore Dunstan*? The *Grunchies* King?!

MARGO. (*Takes drink from him.*) I don't know why you're acting so surprised! Sagamore is kind, and loving, and considerate—

TONY. And loaded.

MARGO. His money has nothing to do with it!

TONY. You'd marry him if he were poor?

MARGO. Of course!

TONY. Then why not re-marry *me*? *I'm* poor! (*Before she can retort, he adds:*) And I wouldn't have a heart seizure on the honeymoon!

MARGO. Tony, Sagamore is *not* that *old*!

TONY. Maggie, that guy was in graduate school with your grandfather!

MARGO. That's a lie! Oh, all right, he *was*, but they weren't contemporaries! I mean, Gramps went *back* to school after his business was established, to *complete* his education! There must be—at least—more than—*ten years'* difference in their ages!

TONY. Oh, forgive me! *That* only makes him slightly older than your *father*!

MARGO. And what does *age* matter, anyhow? It's what a man *is* that counts! Sagamore has never once *mentioned* the difference in our ages!

TONY. *Only* because he can't spare the *time*! (*As she reacts and tries to think of a comeback, he suddenly laughs.*)

MARGO. (*Fuming.*) *I* don't think it was so funny!

TONY. That's *not* what I was laughing at. It just occurred to me what a great couple you two will make— "Maggie and Saggie"!

MARGO. (*Coldly.*) It's so easy to make fun of a man you've never met!

TONY. Well then, isn't it about time you paraded him over here? I mean, your *father* had to look *me* over before the wedding — don't *I* get the same privilege before surrendering the franchise?

MARGO. Do you know — it would serve you right!

TONY. What would?

MARGO. Meeting Sagamore — seeing all those marvelous qualities that you happen to lack — finding out what makes a man *really* attractive to a woman!

TONY. Aw, Maggie —

MARGO. No, this was *your* idea, and the more I think of it, the more I like it! Maybe it would get you off this nobility kick — I'd hate to have you go through life thinking I was withering away with a candidate for Senile City!

TONY. Okay! Bring him! Maybe it will teach me a lesson!

MARGO. Maybe it will, at that! Okay, buster, you're on! Name the day!

TONY. (*Pointing down toward threshold of door.*) It depends how long it takes me to build a ramp for his wheelchair!

MARGO. Listen, kiddo, Sagamore's in a lot better shape than *you* are! He plays golf, and tennis, and squash — !

TONY. Lucky you! He'll hardly be home at all!

MARGO. Can't face up to it, can you! Can't admit there just *might* be another male with attractions you never dreamed of!

TONY. Okay, Maggie, you're on! How about tonight?! Haul him over here!

MARGO. Tonight? . . . That's — rather short notice —

TONY. Oh, that's right, he'll have to get in shape to climb the stairs!

MARGO. You lousy rat! All right! Tonight it is! Once he gets a look at you, he may marry me out of sympathy!

TONY. Glad to speed things up for you! Grab him while he lasts!

MARGO. Damn right I will! (*Drains her drink, chokes.*) I thought you said eighty proof?!

TONY. (*Patting her on back.*) You're just not used to it without ice.

MARGO. (*Pulls away from him, hands him empty glass.*) What time do you want us — unless you were bluffing?

TONY. Bluffing? Never! The least the ex-husband can do is fling an engagement party for his departing wife! I may even wear a tie!

MARGO. (*With a glance at his thongs and otherwise bare feet.*) Shoes and socks will be sufficient.

TONY. Won't that be a little drafty? (*She gives him a scathing look, and he relents.*) Oh, don't worry. I wouldn't want to come in second-best to your breakfast-food buddy! Unless, after business hours, he goes Hawaiian?

MARGO. Don't be snide! For your information, Sagamore just made the best-dressed list! I have never seen him without a suit on!

TONY. Well, *that's* a mercy!

MARGO. Tony — !

TONY. Okay-okay, truce! (*Raises his glass.*) Here's to the happy couple — may you both be as happy in your marriage as — (*With less bravado.*) — as I was in mine. (*Drains his glass, will move to cabinet and set empty glasses on top of it, during her speech.*)

MARGO. (*Miserable.*) Tony — be fair — *I* was happy, too. There were *plenty* of good times — unforgettable moments — marvelous memories —

TONY. (*Turns to face her.*) Then why the hell — ?!

MARGO. There just weren't *enough* of them!

TONY. I didn't know we were operating on a quota system.

MARGO. Please, Tony, Don't. I don't have any fight left in me. Let's be friends. What time tonight do you want us?

TONY. (*Clasps her hand fondly.*) Oh, hell—I don't know—eight-thirty, I guess—no, better make it nearer nine—I've got to go out for party food and booze—unless your tycoon would prefer a bowl of Grunchies?

MARGO. (*Laughs.*) Tony, Sagamore just *makes* the stuff—he's got more sense than to actually *eat* it!

TONY. Can I quote you on that?

MARGO. Don't you dare! (*Tries to withdraw from his still-maintained grasp.*) Now, may I please have my hand back? I'd hate to leave without it.

TONY. (*All jollity vanished, speaking from the heart.*) Maggie—don't go—for the love of God, don't go!

MARGO. (*Trying to fight her own emotions, averts her gaze.*) Tony—please—I—

TONY. (*Pulls her to him with his free arm.*) I don't know where we went wrong—where *I* went wrong—but there's got to be a way to make it right again—!

MARGO. Tony—

TONY. Maybe if we talked—

MARGO. Stop—

TONY. Just sat down and talked—

MARGO. This is crazy—

TONY. We never did talk, you know, not really—

MARGO. My life's all planned and decided—

TONY. I didn't even know we had a *problem* till the day you walked out—

MARGO. I've just regained my equilibrium—

TONY. Listen—we could do it—I could change—just tell me what to do—give me a fighting chance—

MARGO. Oh, Tony—I—I don't know—

TONY. There's never been anyone but you—from the first day I set eyes on you—

MARGO. I can't think straight—

TONY. (*Has been holding her nearer and nearer, now embraces her with both arms.*) There never could be anyone else for me—you're my whole life, my whole world—

MARGO. You're mixing me up—

TONY. *Please* stay—stay and talk things out—we had something pretty special once, didn't we—?!

MARGO. I—well—yes, we did, but—

TONY. We could find it again—find our way back—

MARGO. (*Her arms going around him, tentatively.*) Could we? *Could* we?

TONY. If we could just discuss it—calmly—just the two of us—

MARGO. But we *tried* that—!

TONY. Sure, with two lawyers and a marriage counselor breathing down our necks—and that was already *after* the breakup, we were both hurt and miserable and defensive—we weren't ourselves—!

MARGO. Oh, Tony—! (*They are millimeters from a kiss; then there is a KNOCK at the door, and even as they react and move apart in surprise, the door opens and* IRV—*wearing only a wraparound towel and shower clogs—steps into the room, on:*)

IRVING. Hey, Tony, do you mind if I use your shower—? Oh! Margo! You're still here! I thought—

MARGO. (*Since the Magic Moment is now shattered.*) Never mind, I was just leaving, anyhow.

TONY. (*Grabs her arm.*) No you weren't.

IRVING. Listen, I can come back *later* for that shower—

TONY. Irving, *what* is this endless *yen* you have for my *plumbing*?!

IRVING. Forgot to pay my water bill. But if I'd known Margo was still here—

MARGO. Will you stop jabbering and get into that shower?! Pee-*yoo*! (*Grimaces and takes a backstep from him.*)

IRVING. I don't really have to—

MARGO. *Oh* yes you do! (*Fans air between them in showerward direction.*) And hurry!

IRVING. (*Starts toward platform.*) This is all my fault—see, when I heard the door close twice—

TONY. (*Too anxious to be rid of him to realize or remember what that statement means.*) Will you *go*?! Maggie and I are having a *very* important discussion!

MARGO. Tony, be reasonable! With Irving here, how can we possibly—

TONY. He's not *going* to be here! (*Gets behind* IRV *and starts pushing him toward platform.*) Get *into* that shower and don't come out till I *send* for you!

IRVING. (*Continuing move under his own power.*) I could get awfully pruny—

TONY. (*Even as* IRV *exits toward the bathroom.*) Now please, Maggie, if we can get back to—

MARGO. Hold on a second—what did Irving mean about hearing your door close twice?

TONY. (*Impatiently.*) Oh, hell, it's just that earlier he told me he'd wait till you'd gone, then come back here for a drink. What he probably heard was—was— (*Realizes, wide-eyed, whirls and lurches toward platform.*) Irv! Wait! You can't take that shower!

IRVING. (*Off.*) Stop worrying! I'll never hear you two with the water running.

TONY. (*On platform now, hand on rail, shouting bathroomward.*) That's not the point!

MARGO. Tony, *why* are you acting so *nervous*?

TONY. (*As he whirls to face her, frantic.*) I'm not *acting*! I mean—not *nervous*! (*Whirls back archwayward and shrills in panic:*) Irv, you *can't* take that *shower!*

IRVING. (*Off.*) Of course I can! What's the problem? (*We can hear his voice varying suitably to his actions:*) I open the bathroom door . . . step inside . . . drop my towel . . . open the shower-curtain—(*We hear a loud SCREAM from* CORAL, *overlapped immediately by a similar loud SCREAM from* IRV; TONY *and* MARGO *both react, and while she is more startled than suspicious, he rushes back across the room to her, starts dragging her toward door, babbling in frantic invention:*)

TONY. It's too *noisy* to talk in here! Quick, out in the hall—!

MARGO. (*Resisting his tugging, still merely startled.*) Tony, what was that *screaming*?!

TONY. The water's like *ice!*

MARGO. But I heard *two* voices!

TONY. The bathroom has an *echo!* (*NOTE: The off-stage scream-duet has been continuing over the preceding speeches, but* CORAL's *half of the duet now becomes an* onstage *scream as she rushes in through arch-way, minus her dress, clad in shoes, shockings and slip, and gallops straight across the room into* TONY's *unwilling embrace, while* MARGO *reacts with wide-eyed fury.*)

TONY. Coral, will you stop screaming?!

CORAL. But there's a maniac in there! (*Reacts to* MARGO.) Oh. *Hel*lo!

MARGO. (*Turns, reaches for doorknob.*) Hel*lo* and goodbye!

TONY. (*Manages to grab her arm, and haul her back to him, while still holding a squirming* CORAL *with his free arm.*) Wait! Stop! I can explain!

MARGO. (*Pulls free, whirls to face him.*) You have ten seconds!

TONY. Coral—please—tell her why you're *here!*

MARGO. Why you're here *dressed* like that!

TONY. No, *just* why you're here! (*During following,* IRV *will enter uneasily through archway, his towel once more around him, holding the shredded dress out of which* CORAL *obviously tore free limply in one hand, and just stand on platform, trying his best to be casual.*)

CORAL. Well, see, when Tony didn't show up last night at Munchkinland—

MARGO. (*Incredulous.*) *Where*?

TONY. Munchkinland! The club where she works! All the waiters are midgets!

IRVING. (*Fascinated.*) Really?

CORAL. (*Sees him, clutches* TONY *even tighter.*) It's the flasher!

TONY. Will you let *go* of me and tell my wife why you're *here*?!

CORAL. (*Still holding him.*) I thought she was your *ex*-wife.

MARGO. I am—and apparently with good reason!

TONY. Oh, cut it out! If *you* can find a new romance, why can't *I*?!

CORAL. (*Squeals with delight, holds him tighter.*) Oh, Tony!

TONY. (*To* MARGO, *frantically.*) That was a hypothetical question!

CORAL. (*Disappointed.*) Oh, Tony!

MARGO. (*To* TONY) So I'm the only woman you ever loved—your whole life—your whole world!

TONY. Maggie, there is *nothing* between me and Coral!

MARGO. Oh, *come* now, she's still got her *slip* on!

TONY. (*Still facing* MARGO, *thrusts* CORAL *away from him.*) She is here on *business*!

MARGO. Who's arguing!

TONY. *My* business!

MARGO. Are you trying to tell me *this* is Old White Hair in that Rocking Chair?!

TONY. Maggie, my relationship with Coral has nothing to do with Mother's Day!

MARGO. (*Starts for door again.*) Tell me something I *don't* know! (*Opens door.*)

TONY. (*Despondently.*) Are you still coming to the party?

MARGO. (*Whirls in doorway to face him, about to explode—then she pauses, considers a second, and:*) Damn right I am! I *want* Sagamore to meet you! I want him to *see* the ghastly fate he's *saving* me from!

TONY. Then let's *hope* he doesn't forget to wear his *glasses*!

MARGO. (*Slams door.*) He doesn't *wear* glasses!

TONY. Well, you can always *describe* me to him!

MARGO. I mean he doesn't *need* them! (*Then, with less assurance.*) That is—oh, maybe for reading small print—

TONY. On the Geritol bottle.

MARGO. (*Finds she is fighting a laugh, and not succeeding well.*) Now—stop that—your constant harping on his age—just because he's—a little older—

TONY. Is that a *smile* I see squirming onto those luscious lips?

MARGO. N-nonsense! And—and he *never* takes Geritol! Never!

TONY. Can't lift the spoon? (*This time the laugh comes; she tries to conceal it, turning away from him, but he sees his advantage and presses it—except that his "rare gift", somewhat spoils the moment:*) There, that's better! Don't you see? You belong with a man like me!

MARGO. (*Stiffens instantly, all amusement gone, whirls on him.*) See?! See what you did? If you think I can live my life with *that*—!

TONY. (*All flustered and terrified and apologetic.*) No, wait! I didn't think! Hold on—give me a chance—if I swear to you—give my solemn vow—do my darnedest *never* to do such a thing *again* as long I live—!

MARGO. (*Quietly, sadly.*) It wouldn't work. You'd mean it, I know. But you couldn't keep your promise. Something *really* important would be under discussion, and all at once you'd be communicating in *couplets*! (*Pulls door open.*) I'm sorry, Tony, but—enough is enough! (*Starts out.*)

IRVING. Margo, no!

CORAL. Please don't go!

TONY. (*Even as a hesitant* MARGO *seni-turns back to face him.*) Not when I adore you so! (*Then* TRIO *winces, realizing they've united unwittingly to do the very thing* TONY *had just vowed not to, as* MARGO *give a weary little sigh, and:*)

MARGO. I rest my case. (*Exits to hall, closing door after her;* TRIO *just stands there for a long moment, defeated; then:*)

IRVING. (*With rueful encouragement.*) You can always sell it to Hallmark . . .

TONY. (*Despairingly.*) Listen, buddy, if I could sell to Hallmark, would I be living in a dump like this?!

CORAL. "Buddy"? you mean this guy's *not* a sex maniac?

TONY. (*Shrugs.*) He's a student at UCLA. *You* decide.

CORAL. (*Scanning* IRV.) Isn't he a little *old* to be in college?

TONY. We're *all* a little old right now.

IRVING. Aw, c'mon, Tony! How the hell did *I* know

you had a *dame* stashed in your shower?!

CORAL. "Dame"?!

IRVING. (*Pontifically.*) In England, that is a title of honor!

CORAL. No wonder they lost the Revolution! (*To* TONY.) Hey, who *is* this fresh-air freak, anyhow?

TONY. (*Distracted from his misery.*) Oh, I'm sorry—Irving Moss—Coral Kelly.

IRVING. "Coral"? Like that stuff they dredge up out of the sea?

CORAL. "Moss"? Like that stuff on the damp side of a rock?

TONY. I knew you two would hit it off.

IRVING. (*Approaching* CORAL, *extending remnants of dress.*) Oh, here. Sorry about ripping it.

TONY. Why *did* you, anyhow?

IRVING. (*As* CORAL *takes dress, starts inspecting it.*) Hell, she was screaming up a storm—trying to run out of the room—I knew Margo was out here—so I tried to help.

CORAL. Well, thank heaven it's not torn—just a seam gave way. Tony, do you have a needle and thread?

IRVING. I have. Down the hall in my apartment. In fact, I may even have a dress in your size!

CORAL. (*Backsteps from him, suspiciously.*) How's that again?

IRVING. (*Insulted.*) It just so happens one of my minors was dressmaking.

CORAL. If you think *that* eases my mind about you, you're crazy! (*PHONE RINGS.*)

TONY. (*Moving toward it.*) *Now* what?!

IRVING. With your luck, the I.R.S. is going to audit your tax returns, the police want you for questioning, and you've just been drafted.

TONY. (*At phone.*) And *that's* probably the *good*

news! (*Picks up phone.*) Hello? . . . Lucille! . . . What?! But you can't! I mean — the stuff is in the mail, and — . . . But why should I lie to you? . . . Oh . . . I have? . . . I didn't realize . . . Oh, boy . . . Yeah . . . Yeah, I understand . . . Thanks, I really appreciate it . . . Sure, sure, I'll have it . . . Oh, but could you make it before nine o'clock — I'm having some people in, and — . . . Yeah . . .Yeah, thanks. You're a doll. (*Hangs up, sags, covers face with both hands.*) Oh, damn, damn, *damn*, damn, damn!

IRVING. (*As he and* CORAL *move sympathetically down to* TONY.) Your luck is running as usual?

TONY. (*Uncovers face wearily.*) That was Lucille Larrabee, the gal who edits my copy. I owe her a whole backlog of stuff — Mother's Day, Christmas, Halloween. She's stopping by to get it, tonight.

CORAL. So what's the problem?

TONY. I don't *have* it! *None* of it! I tried to con her earlier, telling her it was on its way in the mail, but she didn't buy it. She says my output has been slipping badly since Margo walked out, and she suspected I was hedging about my progress. But if I have the stuff when she comes by, she'll cover for me with the publisher.

CORAL. Sounds like your job's on the line.

TONY. Is it ever! And it's gonna be tough enough wooing Margo back even *with* my lousy job — if I don't even *have* a job — !

CORAL. (*Interrupts.*) So *write* the stuff for her!

TONY. *When*?! She says she'll be in the neighborhood about eight-thirty. If I work like crazy, I can probably have it all written — but how do I do my shopping and get ready for the party, besides?!

IRVING. Have no fears, buddy. *I'll* do your shopping. *And* fix the canapes and everything else you need.

TONY. Oh, Irv — *would* you?

CORAL. More important — *can* you?

IRVING. Nothing simpler. I also minored in Domestic Science. You haven't lived till you've tased my Nut Fudgies!

CORAL. A dressmaker *and* a chef? You're going to make some woman a wonderful wife!

IRVING. Say, while we're on that subject — are you married?

CORAL. (*Takes a backstep.*) Now, hold on there, Chubby — !

TONY. Irv, this is no time to —

IRVING. It's *perfect* timing! Look, here I am, face to face with the most gorgeous girl I ever met in my entire life, and Grandfather Moss's will has a *sub*-clause that if I get *married* my endowment doubles — !

CORAL. (*Moves nearer to* TONY, *nervously.*) Tony, what is your fat friend talking about — ?!

TONY. He gets twenty thousand bucks a year till he completes his education.

IRVING. (*Moves nearer* CORAL.) *Forty* thousand with *you* at my side!

CORAL. (*Jumps around* TONY *to keep him between her and* IRV.) *This* guy is a *nut*!

TONY. Irv, will you lay off?!

IRVING. But this is the chance of a lifetime!

TONY. What about all those coeds who are so crazy about you? Can't you marry one of *them*?

IRVING. Of *course* not! Whatever their dating talents, they're in college to get an education! As soon as they got their degree they'd *leave* me!

TONY. What makes you think *Coral* wouldn't?

IRVING. She's not *interested* in college! She could concentrate on *me*!

CORAL. You're out of your mind!

IRVING. Only with love for you! Just think what a gorgeous name you'd end up with—"Coral Moss"!

CORAL. (*Starts edging doorward.*) I'm getting out of here!

IRVING. Aw, c'mon! Forty thousand a year is nothing to sneeze at!

CORAL. I'm sorry, but I have this thing about dating undergraduates—!

TONY. Listen, *both* of you—!

IRVING. (*Ignoring him.*) Coral, *think*! *Any* woman could marry a doctor or a lawyer or an engineer—I'm offering *you* the chance to marry a doctor *and* a lawyer *and* an engineer!

CORAL. Tony—he doesn't just *talk* crazy—he *is* crazy! I thought his *waistline* was chubby—but it's *nothing* compared to the fat in his *head*!

TONY. Relax, Coral. Irv just minors in anything that hasn't been booked solid every semester.

CORAL. (*To* IRV.) What are you studying to *be*?

TONY. The world's oldest living student.

CORAL. (*Sizing* IRV *up.*) I think he's *already* reached *that* plateau.

IRVING. I'm younger than I look!

CORAL. You'd *have* to be!

TONY. Hey, *hold* it, you two—what *is* all this?

IRVING. Well, she started it—screaming in my face that way!

CORAL. I suppose my first glimpse of *you* was *soothing*?!

IRVING. It's a habit of mine never to get into a shower stall with my clothes on—which is more than I can say for *some* people!

CORAL. I was hiding from his wife!

IRVING. Why? You and Tony aren't up to anything! . . . Are you?

CORAL. Of course not! Our relationship is strictly on a *cash* basis!

TONY. I'm glad you didn't say *that* to Margo!

IRVING. But it was only a matter of time!

CORAL. Oh, keep your shirt on!

TONY. *What* shirt?!

IRVING. Don't blame me! I didn't know this was Ladies Day in your shower!

CORAL. Oh, go soak your head!

IRVING. That's what I was *trying* to do!

TONY. Hold it! Everybody! So we were *all* a little stupid, okay?

CORAL. Okay!

IRVING. Okay!

TONY. (*As soon as* ALL *seem to get their emotional bearings again.*) Now that we're all calmed down—(*Abruptly almost in tears.*) What the hell am I going to *do*?!

IRVING. I don't know what *you're* going to do, but *I* need a *shower*!

CORAL. You're telling *me*!

IRVING. Oh, go sing to your midgets!

CORAL. Sing what? Tony never wrote my new material!

TONY. I was too busy wrecking my life!

IRVING. It's not wrecked *yet*, buddy—Margo *said* she was coming back!

TONY. Sure, with her new fiance!

IRVING. You can always poison the chip dip.

CORAL. Oh, go scrub your armpits before you start a smog alert!

TONY. Wait! Irv—you've just given me a great idea!

CORAL. Tony, are you crazy? Poisoned chip dip is Murder One!

TONY. No-no, I don't mean that—I mean the stuff

I'm going to serve at the party!

IRVING. You're not having chip dip?

TONY. Of course I am!

CORAL. Then what—?

TONY. (*Interrupts.*) I mean the *kind* of stuff I'll serve! Look, this guy is way over the hill—he's got to wear dentures—maybe has an ulcer—or he's on a salt-free diet—

IRVING. Tony, that's *it*! You serve caramels, beef jerky, hot peppers, lots of salty stuff—potato chips, anchovies, caviar, pretzels, fritos, peanut butter—!

CORAL. Irving, that's a hell of a combination for *anyone* to swallow! I'm getting thirsty just *listening* to it!

IRVING. Yeah, it *would* raise Tony's water bill!

TONY. That's never bothered you *before*!

CORAL. Hold it—I just realized—if he doesn't *tolerate* that kind of stuff, he just won't *eat* any.

TONY. Oh, damn, she's right.

IRVING. No! Hold it! I've got it—the one thing that he's *got* to eat if you serve it!

TONY AND CORAL. What?

IRVING. *Grunchies*! (TONY *and* CORAL *whoop with glee—then* TONY *stops, shaking his head, which sobers* CORAL *into sympathetic curiousity.*)

CORAL. There's a *flaw* in the plan?

TONY. Yeah. Nobody serves breakfast cereal at a party!

IRVING. But Tony—you don't serve it *as* cereal!

TONY. What do you mean?

IRVING. You use it as the *base* of your canapes! Olives stuffed with Grunchies!

CORAL. (*Catching on, enthused.*) Grunchie-and-walnut clusters!

IRVING. French-fried Grunchies!

CORAL. Grunchie aspic!

IRVING. Grunchie-and-cheese on a toothpick!

TONY. It's brilliant! It can't fail! His own product—he'll *have* to try some of everything! His dentures will *scream* to be taken out! I'll get Margo back yet!

IRVING. Thanks to a little nutpick—

TONY. A little toothpick—

CORAL. And a little aspic! (BOTH *stare at her; she jams her fists onto her hips.*) You know *very well* what I mean!

IRVING. Sorry. (*Then, to* TONY.) I wish I could be here to see it!

CORAL. So come to the party!

TONY. Hey, may *I* keep control of the guest list?

IRVING. You mean I'm not welcome?

TONY. Only if you smell like a human being!

IRVING. (*Starts for bathroom.*) I can take a hint!

CORAL. (*As* IRV *exits.*) Gee, Tony, I wish I didn't have to work tonight—I'd come by, too, and give you moral support.

TONY. That's—damn nice of you, Coral.

CORAL. I'm a rather nice person—if some people would take the time to notice.

TONY. Aw, Coral . . .

CORAL. It's all right. I understand.

TONY. It's *nothing* about you, *personally*, Coral—

CORAL. I just came into your life one wedding too late. (*Sighs, starts to open door, looks down at herself.*) Oh, damn, I can't go out on the street like this!

TONY. Irv's apartment is the second door on the left. He wasn't kidding about his closet—take what you need, and leave that dress for him to repair for you.

CORAL. How do I get in?

TONY. It's not locked.

CORAL. How do you know?

TONY. (*With an isn't-it-obvious? shrug:*) He can't *possibly* have his *key* with him! Unless he's got it strung around him under the towel.

CORAL. He hasn't. And don't remind me how I know! (*Starts out, pausing on threshold for:*) Now, come on, cheer up. You've got a wife to win back. Start making those Grunchie-chewies and keep your chin up. And remember, whatever you do, *stop* talking to Margo in *couplets*!

TONY. (*Laughs.*) Couplets? No way, not a chance! Nothing's gonna wreck *my* romance! (*And as he grimaces, realizing he's done it again, and* CORAL *shakes her head ruefully and starts out the door, her torn dress flung serape-fashion over one shoulder—.*)

THE CURTAIN FALLS

ACT II

*That night about eight-thirty. Drapes have been drawn
closed at upstage window. Bottles of liquor, a tray
with glasses, and a bucket of ice are atop the
cabinet. Screen masks kitchen area.*

At curtain-rise, we find TONY *at the desk. He now wears
shoes and socks, and cheery slacks and short-
sleeved sport shirt. There is a stack of completed
pages beside the typewriter, and he is typing deter-
minedly and very fast, his total concentration on
the page in the typewriter. There is a KNOCK at the
door.*

TONY. (*Stops typing, looks at his watch, calls toward
door.*) Who's there?

IRVING. (*Off.*) The caterer! Open the damned door!

TONY. (*Torn between continuing his work and moving to door.*) It *is* open!

IRVING. (*Off.*) The hell it is! I can't reach the
doorknob!

TONY. Oh . . . damn it! (*Gets up, hurries to door,
flings it open, and starts right back toward desk, where
he will sit again.*) Come in, come in, I'm busy! (*Resumes
typing away at page as* IRV *comes in; he is garbed akin
to* TONY.)

IRVING. (*Carrying portable phonograph, with records
on the spindle, and a stack of bowls balanced
precariously on top.*) Aren't you finished *yet*?! (*Will
manage to get to dinette table and disencumber himself,
over dialogue.*) You said you only had one page to go!

TONY. This is the page! Now stop interrupting me!

IRVING. (*Will pick up bowls from atop turntable and*

43

vanish behind screen with them, during:) I work, I slave, I clean the apartment, I cook my fingers to the bone—!

TONY. (*Typing like mad.*) Nag, nag, nag!

IRVING. (*Emerges minus bowls, moves down to stand right of* TONY.) How's it coming? That Larrabee dame's due any minute.

TONY. (*Stops typing long enough for:*) Who knows! I've been too busy *writing* it to *evaluate* it!

IRVING. (*Lifts topsheet from stack, reads aloud:*) "Though the blizzard has knocked transportation to hell, no plane, no train, no bus . . . Noel!" (*Shakes head, replaces sheet atop stack.*) And a Merry Christmas to you, too!

TONY. (*Stops typing, shrugs.*) I ran out of rhymes for "Ho-ho-ho!"

IRVING. (*Searching through stack, curiously.*) How'd you make out with Mother's Day—?

TONY. (*Guiltily.*) Oh . . . not too bad. Here, you don't want to read that junk—! (*Tries to take sheet from* IRV, *but misses it.*)

IRVING. (*Looks at sheet, raises his eyebrows, reads aloud:*) "As you sit there in your rocker with your hair becoming white, spread some cheese upon a crocker, 'cause it's Mother's Day tonight!" (*Transfixes* TONY *with a look of betrayal.*)

TONY. (*Pulls sheet out of his hand.*) I was desperate, okay?! (*Slaps it back onto pile.*)

IRVING. How much is my commission?

TONY. Aw, Irv—!

IRVING. Come on, buddy—cut me in, and I'll give you a dandy rhyme for "arthritis"!

TONY. Who says I need one?

IRVING. (*Shrugs.*) Well, with white hair in a rocking chair, it's only a matter of time!

TONY. (*Turns away, resumes typing.*) Oh, go cook your Grunchies and stop being funny! I've got to get finished, I need the money! (*Stops typing, slumps, covers his face.*)

IRVING. Tony, you're doing it again!

TONY. (*Uncovers face, angry and miserable.*) It's hard not to use my poetic powers after thinking in rhyme for the past seven hours! (*Reacts, groans, shakes head.*)

IRVING. (*Takes hold of back of swivel chair — which has a wheeled base — and pulls* TONY *on it firmly upstage away from the desk.*) Enough is enough! Let Lucille settle for what you've got!

TONY. But Irv —!

IRVING. Think about Margo! One little couplet and she goes right out that door, forever!

TONY. (*Stands up from chair, points toward typewriter.*) But there's just one card to go — as soon as I think of a rhyme —!

IRVING. (*Rolls chair past* TONY *to desk, sits in it himself.*) Hell, let *me* finish it for you! I also minored in Ogden Nash!

TONY. But it's only one line —!

IRVING. *I'll* do it! You practice thinking in prose! (*Scans page.*) Let's see what you've got here — (*Reads aloud.*) "Goldilocks suits you, with your soft blonde hair —" . . . (*To* TONY.) What's the occasion?

TONY. (*Glumly.*) Halloween.

IRVING. Aha! Then I've got it! (*Types rapidly, smiles in triumph, pulls page from typewriter.*) There you are, buddy! Your job is secure again!

TONY. (*Reads page, raises eyebrows.*) Irv — I'm not sure about this — I mean, *kids* buy these cards!

IRVING. Don't worry, they'll never catch the extra meaning.

TONY. (*Setting page atop the stack.*) It'll have to do, I've run out of time! (*Brightens.*) Hey, I'm improving—that didn't rhyme! . . . Oops.

IRVING. (*Gets up, claps a sympathetic hand on* TONY's *shoulder.*) You've got to *think* before you speak, or you'll leave your love-life up the creek! (*Reacts, pulls his hand from* TONY's *shoulder, takes a backstep.*) Good grief, it's contagious! (*Starts for door, fast.*) You'd better get ready for your love-in—I've got Grunchies in the oven! (*Stops with hand on doorknob.*) Did I just say what I thought I said?

TONY. (*Speaking carefully, moves toward him.*) Don't panic. I'm sure it's just temporary. There, see? *I* did it, and if I can do it, so can you.

IRVING. You're right. We're psyching ourselves out. Anyone can rhyme by accident.

TONY. (*Ruminating.*) "By accident . . . by accident"—Nope, you're wrong. Nobody could rhyme that.

IRVING. (*While opening door.*) Listen, I've got Grunchie-stuff in your refrigerator—while I'm getting the stuff out of my oven, start putting it into those bowls I brought over, okay?

TONY. (*Starts toward screen.*) Check. And hurry back—I need moral support.

IRVING. (*Starts out.*) Well, hold down the fort!

TONY. You did it again!

IRVING. I did? When? (*Realizes, looks at* TONY, *then* BOTH *shake their heads wearily, and* IRV *exits to hall, shutting door after him, and* TONY *moves out of sight behind screen; then we know he has opened the refrigerator because we see light and a sort of shadowy movement on the translucent folding-screen, though he is too far upstage of the screen for his silhouette to ap-*

pear in any recognizable detail; then light and shadow disappear as he closes door, and reappears, emptyhanded, and moves down toward cabinet, on:)

TONY. (*To himself.*) Spoons—I need spoons! (*Gets to cabinet and is just about to open it when there is a KNOCK at the door; he moves to door.*) Who is it?

LUCILLE. (*Off.*) Lucille!

TONY. (*In act of opening door.*) Hey, great, you're right on time! (LUCILLE LARRABEE, *middle-fortyish, rather pretty, on the tall-and-thin side, and wearing a light mid-calf-length topcoat, and a large—very oversized—bright red bow atop her head, enters on her line:*)

LUCILLE. You must have the copy, or you wouldn't be so cheerful!

TONY. (*Takes her elbow, guides her deskward.*) Every line of it! And don't think I don't appreciate what you're doing for me. I need this job, bad.

LUCILLE. Let's hope the copy lets you keep it! (*Picks top sheet off pile.*) What's this one for?

TONY. Oh, That. That's—uh—for Halloween. But please don't judge the rest of the stuff by that one—it's—uh—not my usual style.

LUCILLE. (*Puzzled, scans sheet and reads aloud:*) "Goldilocks suits you, with your soft blonde hair—but I'd rather see you a little bear!" (*Turns to him, wide-eyed.*) Tony—!

TONY. (*Guiltily.*) I know, I know, but believe me, the *rest* aren't like *that*!

LUCILLE. Oh, I hope you're wrong!

TONY. (*Reacts.*) "Wrong"?!

LUCILLE. (*Waves sheet in his face.*) Tony, this is brilliant! None of your usual namby-pamby sweetness-and-light! This one is gonna *sell*! It's got zing—it's got power — it's even a little *spicy*! (*Pulls desk chair out.*) I can hardly wait to get to the rest!

TONY. Lucille, you're not going to read all that copy *now* — ?!

LUCILLE. (*Moving to sit in chair.*) Listen, it won't take long, and the sooner I read it, the sooner I can put your mind at ease about your job. (*Sets paper on desk.*)

TONY. Well — if you put it that way — (*Shrugs, extends arms.*) Here, I may as well take your coat. . . .

LUCILLE. (*Still standing, starts undoing coat buttons.*) Oh, thanks, that's a good idea. I hope *all* the new stuff is as good as the Goldilocks rhyme — that's almost as funny as your Grunchies Jingle!

TONY. My *what*?

LUCILLE. (*Still unbuttoning.*) Don't you remember — about two months back — that jingle contest — ?

TONY. Lucille, that was a joke! I was just steamed about the divorce, and wanted to show Margo I could write something besides greeting-cards! But it came out so bad, I'd never have submitted it.

LUCILLE. (*On final button.*) That's what I thought. So I submitted it for you.

TONY. (*Reacts, turns her to face him.*) Lucille, you didn't!

LUCILLE. But why not?

TONY. If Margo ever saw it, it'd be the last straw! Bad enough we didn't get along domestically — if I capped it by making fun of her job — !

LUCILLE. Tony, I don't get it?! I thought you and Margo were washed up.

TONY. Well, we're *not*! At least — I hope not. There's still a fighting chance — that's who's coming over tonight — Margo — and her fiance.

LUCILLE. How cozy! Or is *that* the "fighting chance"

you meant? You're going to punch the guy out?

TONY. Well, *hardly*! Sagamore Dunstan is old enough to be my grandfather!

LUCILLE. The Grunchies King?! *He's* old enough to be *anybody's* grandfather! What's she marrying him for—wheelchair lessons?

TONY. For all *I* know! . . . Here, give me that coat! (*She turns her back, undoes last button, and he takes her coat, turns, and starts with it for closet, not seeing—as we do immediately—that she is clad only in a sort of tassel-and-bangle-covered bathing-suit kind of thing; he will proceed to closet, open door, step in, hang up coat, turn around, come out, shut door, and only then will he react to her outfit—all this over following dialogue:*) I *do* wish you hadn't submitted that jingle, Lucille—I wrote it from a heart full of hate!

LUCILLE. (*Takes page from stack.*) Frankly, I thought it was a little masterpiece—hate or no hate!

TONY. I can't *afford* a masterpiece right now! I'd win the contest and lose my wife!

LUCILLE. But—if you *won*, it would mean the Grunchies people *liked* your jingle.

TONY. (*Just coming out of closet.*) Margo *knows* how I feel about Grunchies! She'd know I did it as a gag—she'd *hear* the hate between the lines—she'd never speak to me again—! (*Has door shut, is starting across room toward her.*) So let's hope that thing went right into the trash can as soon as they saw it, and— (*Sees what she's wearing, stops in shocked disbelief.*) Yipe!

LUCILLE. (*Can see what he's reacting to, looks down at herself.*) What's the matter?

TONY. (*Pulls out of paralysis, rushes to her.*) "What's the matter"?! Lucille! That outfit!

LUCILLE. Don't you like it?

TONY. Not with *Margo* due here any minute! What the hell kind of a getup do you call *that*? Do you *always* dress like this after business hours?

LUCILLE. Well, of *course* not! But there's a go-go-dancing contest over at Munchkinland tonight, and I'm meeting some girl friends there — we thought it would be fun to try out.

TONY. But if Margo sees you — !

LUCILLE. I'll just *tell* her I'm on my way to *Munchkinland*!

TONY. (*Panic-stricken.*) You can't! She'll never believe it — not twice in one day!

LUCILLE. Twice in one day?

TONY. (*Dragging her closetward.*) I've got to get you *out* of here!

LUCILLE. (*Resisting, flailing a hand deskward.*) But I haven't finished reading your copy!

TONY. (*Releases her, rushes toward desk, grabs up papers, on:*) Take it with you! There's no time to spare! Hurry, now, get your coat on!

LUCILLE. (*Catching her infectious urgency, rushes to closet, on:*) All right, all right — but I think you're panicking over nothing! (*There is a KNOCK at the door, and she freezes, drawing in her breath in a terrified gasp.*)

TONY. (*At desk, slumps in despair.*) You were saying? (*Drops papers onto desk, rushes to her.*) Quick, get that topcoat back on!

LUCILLE. Right! (*Yanks open closet door, he rushes past her into closet, she rushes in after him, he comes rushing out with topcoat, extending it as if to help her into it, sees she is not there, and at that point front door starts to open, and he whirls, shuts closet door just as* LUCILLE *reappears from unseen left area of closet in doorway, realizes he is still holding a woman's topcoat, flings it into corner behind the potted plant, and then leans back defensively against closet door, a hideous smile forged on his panicky face; front door, during this, has been swinging open from whatever initial push it was given, but we see nobody on threshold yet — then* IRV, *both hands involved holding a tray covered with platefuls of canapes, steps into room, sees* TONY, *smiles pleasantly.*)

IRVING. Hi! Why didn't you answer the door? (*Will start down to coffeetable with tray, on:*) I had to set this on the floor in the hall and open the door myself!

TONY. Irv! I thought you were Margo! You scared the hell out of me!

IRVING. (*Sets tray on table, starts taking plates off it, setting them out on table.*) What are you so panicky about? You're *expecting* Margo, aren't you?

TONY. (*Steps forward, shoves front door en route so that it swings closed, moves down toward* IRV, *on:*) Yes, but it would have been a *rotten* time for her to arrive, because — (*Behind him, closet door starts to open, and* LUCILLE *starts to come out — and then there is a KNOCK at front door, and she leaps back into closet and shuts door as* TONY *reacts to sound of door-knock.*) Oh, no!

IRVING. (*Too busy with plates to have seen* LUCILLE'S *near-entrance.*) *Relax*, Tony, for pete's sake! What is the *matter* with you?

TONY. (*Dazed, moves toward front door.*) It's a long story — just hope and pray Margo's not wearing a coat! (*Opens door;* MARGO *and* SAGAMORE DUNSTAN — *a tall, silver-haired, well-dressed man in his 60's — are standing there;* BOTH *are wearing topcoats.*) *Yipe!* (*Shuts door in their faces.*)

IRVING. (*Moves up toward him, empty tray in hand.*)

Tony, are you crazy? What are you doing?

TONY. They're *both* wearing coats!

IRVING. (*Continues past* TONY *to closet door.*) So hang them in the closet! (*Takes hold of knob.*)

TONY. I can't!

IRVING. (*Opens closet door, and we see* LUCILLE *standing there.*) Of course you can! (*Turns, sees* LUCILLE, *shuts door instantly.*) No you can't! Tony, who's that *woman* in your closet?!

TONY. Lucille Larrabee!

IRVING. But where are her *clothes*?!

TONY. Those *are* her clothes!

MARGO. (*Off.*) (*KNOCKS as she speaks.*) Tony? . . . Tony! Open the door!

TONY. Quick, get her out of the closet!

IRVING. (*In act of opening closet door again.*) And *then* what — push her out the window?!

LUCILLE. (*Hurries out of closet.*) Tony, maybe if you explain why I'm here —

TONY. Dressed like *that*?!

IRVING. (*Elbow-grabs her, drags her up behind screen, on:*) He's right, they'll *never* believe your story!

LUCILLE. But you haven't *heard* his story!

MARGO. (*Off.*) Tony Dawson, what is the *matter* with you?! (*KNOCKS loudly on door.*)

TONY. (*Leans head close to door as* IRV *shoves* LUCILLE *behind screen.*) Just a minute, the apartment's a mess!

IRVING. (*Rushes down to him, having left tray on range behind screen.*) You've got to get them out of the room so she can get away!

TONY. Right! (*Yanks open door,* MARGO *and* SAGAMORE *step in.*) There, it's all straightened up!

MARGO. (*As* SAGAMORE *helps her out of her coat.*) Your desk is still a mess!

TONY. I think a desk should look lived-in!

IRVING. (*Has come up begind* SAGAMORE, *and helps him out of his coat; he wears a somber business suit and tie.*) Here, let me help you, old man!

MARGO. (*Bridling at his last two words.*) Irving—!

IRVING. I had to call him something! We haven't been introduced!

MARGO. (*Fast and furious.*) Irving Moss—Sagamore Dunstan!

SAGAMORE. (*Extends his hand.*) How do you do!

IRV. (*Drapes coat across* SAGAMORE's *extended forearm.*) Pleased to meet you! Listen, why don't you two go put your coats in on the bed?!

SAGAMORE. Shouldn't I meet her ex-husband first?

TONY. *I'm* her ex-husband!

IRVING. (*Even as* TONY *extends his hand, pushes* SAGAMORE *past him.*) There, you've met! Now go get rid of those coats! Just take 'em back into the bedroom!

SAGAMORE. (*Moves in direction he's been urged,* MARGO *following uncertainly.*) Uh—yes, to be sure! Back in a minute!

IRVING. (*Hurrying toward screen.*) I'll just go see about the canapes! (*Steps begind screen; then, as* MARGO *and* SAGAMORE *exit through archway, he drags* LUCILLE *into view again.*) Quick, open the door, shove her out in the hall!

LUCILLE. But where's my topcoat?

TONY. Oh! Over here! (*Starts to go toward plant, and there is a KNOCK at hall door.*) Yipe! (IRV *shoves* LUCILLE *into still-open closet, shuts door; KNOCK repeats at front door.*)

TONY. Are *you* expecting anybody?

IRVING. Such as *who*? (*Then both look up as* SAGAMORE *and* MARGO, *still carrying their coats, enter and stop upstage of rail.*)

MARGO. Tony . . . You don't *have* a bedroom!

TONY. (*Still in shock.*) I don't? (*Recovers.*) I mean—I *don't*!

SAGAMORE. Then why—?

IRVING. *My* fault! I just *assumed* he had one!

MARGO. (*As she and* SAGAMORE *start back toward closet area.*) Isn't that a coat-closet in the corner?

TONY. (*Leaps backward, spread-eagles himself across closet door.*) *No*!

MARGO. Then where *does* that door lead?

TONY. (*After a panicky moment.*) *Tell* her, Irv!

IRVING. (*Instantly.*) It's his *darkroom*! Can't open the door—all the film would spoil!

SAGAMORE. But—how do you *get* to the film, then?

IRVING. (*Inspired.*) He turns off *all* the lights in *here*, first!

SAGAMORE. Oh. That makes sense.

MARGO. But Tony—when did you get interested in photography?

IRVING. (*Sees* TONY *can't think of a reply, cuts in:*) He was helping me with one of my minors!

SAGAMORE. Tony, that's commendable! I've *often* thought of joining the Big Brothers.

IRVING. You're becoming a monk? (*KNOCK repeats at front door.*)

TONY. You don't understand.

MARGO. Who, Irving or Sagamore?

TONY. Take your pick. (*KNOCK repeats.*)

MARGO. Aren't you going to answer the door?

TONY. No.

MARGO. (*Moves doorward, handing her coat to* TONY *en route.*) You can't just leave a person *standing* out there—! (*Opens door, and there stands* CORAL, *in a flashy sequined dress, holding a miniskirted dress over her arm.*) I take that back. (*Shuts door.*)

SAGAMORE. Margo! Why did you do that?

MARGO. Wellll . . .

TONY. (*Since it's no use anyway.*) Oh, I'll get it! (*Opens door,* CORAL *steps inside quickly.*) Hi! What made *you* decide to pop in?

CORAL. I was afraid the door would slam again.

MARGO. (*Feebly polite.*) My hand slipped.

IRVING. But Coral—why *are* you here? I thought you'd be at work.

CORAL. I didn't want to cross the picket line.

TONY. What picket line?

CORAL. Around *Munchkinland*, of course!

MARGO. The club is closed?

CORAL. Who's gonna *open* it? My *boss* certainly won't!

IRVING. But who's picketing the club?

MARGO. And why?

CORAL. *Waiters*, of course! *Big* waiters! They all look like escapees from Muscle Beach. They say Munchkinland is discriminating against non-midgets!

SAGAMORE. But—your *boss* can't be in the Waiters Union—why won't *he* cross the line!

CORAL. (*Surprised at his obtuseness.*) *Shorty*?!

TONY. Coral, never mind that. We've established why you're not *there*—but why are you *here*?

CORAL. (*Extending garment she carries.*) I just stopped by to return Irv's dress. (SAGAMORE *and* MARGO *react.*)

IRVING. (*Grabs dress from her, fast.*) There was no hurry!

MARGO. Irving—did she say—*your* dress?

CORAL. He's got a closetful of them!

IRVING. (*Lays conciliatory hand on* MARGO'S

shoulder.) But I'm joining the track team next fall!

SAGAMORE. I don't understand—why was this young lady—

TONY. Oh, excuse me! Coral Kelly—Sagamore Dunstan!

CORAL. (*As* SAGAMORE *politely shakes her hand.*) Really? Gee, *you* don't look like *anybody's* grandfather!

SAGAMORE. (*At sea.*) Who said I *did?* (CORAL *immediately turns and points at* TONY, *who is at the same time pointing at* IRV, *who is at the same time pointing at* CORAL, *on:*)

TRIO. Why . . . (*Then* TRIO *realize this is a bad move, and all turn back toward* SAGAMORE *again, ceasing pointing, on:*) *N*obody—!

TONY. (*Still has* MARGO's *coat, now grabs* SAGAMORE's) Here, I'll just hang these in the closet—*darkroom!*

SAGAMORE. But what about your film?

IRVING. Don't worry—I'll get the lights! (*Tosses miniskirt-dress to* TONY *as he passes.*) Here, you'd better put *this* in there, too! (TONY *catches his hint, nods, and* IRV *flips lightswich, and TOTAL BLACKNESS FALLS.*)

CORAL. Tony, *I* didn't know you had a darkroom—?!

IRVING. Of course he has!

CORAL. Where *is* it?

IRVING. We're *in* it! (*Then we see a sliver of light at hall door, as a man in silhouette shoves a woman in silhouette out into hall and shuts door again, restoring blackness.*)

TONY. (*Cheerily.*) Okay, everybody, now we can relax! (*LIGHTS COME ON, and we see smiling* TONY *at switch, no longer holding overcoats [they are in closet] or mini-dress, and* SAGAMORE, CORAL, *and* IRV *blinking at the onslaught of light.*)

SAGAMORE. (*First to notice.*) What's become of Margo—? (*There is a KNOCK at hall door.*)

TONY. (*His smile gone, wearily opens door, and MARGO re-enters, the mini-dress over her arm.*) Hi! What were you doing out *there*?!

MARGO. (*Waves dress.*) Somebody grabbed me, handed me this, and *pushed* me out there!

IRVING. (*An inspired lie.*) That was *me*! I thought you were Coral, and I gave her the dress to put back in my closet!

TONY. (*Relieved, blurts:*) Thanks, old buddy!

MARGO. (*Suspiciously.*) For what?

TONY. (*Quickly.*) For explaining! What else?

CORAL. (*While MARGO is still deciding if she believes him.*) Here, give me the dress and I'll put it back!

TONY / IRVING. *NO*!

SAGAMORE. What's the matter?

MARGO. That's what *I'd* like to know!

TONY. Now, now, what could *possibly* be the matter? Here, give me the dress, and I'll put it in the closet.

MARGO. (*Moves closetward, evading him.*) No-no, let *me*!

TONY. But you can't!

SAGAMORE. Why not?

TONY. Uh—!

IRVING. The film! She'll expose the film! Let me get the lights!

SAGAMORE. I don't understand—*is* that a closet or a *darkroom*?

TONY. Both!

MARGO. (*At closet door.*) We'll just *see* about that! (*And as she turns knob, IRV flips switch, and LIGHTS BLACK OUT, and we hear moving footsteps, and MARGO yelling:*) Hey! (*Then we hear a door slam, and LIGHTS COME UP, and once again we see TONY,*

CORAL, SAGAMORE *and* IRV, *who is just moving from lightswitch;* TONY *still holds mini-dress.*)

SAGAMORE. Margo's gone *again!*

TONY. Yipe! (*Rushes to hall door, yanks it open.*) Nobody there! (*As he turns and closes door again, closet door opens and* MARGO *steps out.*)

MARGO. *Who* shoved me *this* time!?

TONY. (*Miserable, points toward unseen depths of closet.*) Honey, I can explain—!

MARGO. (*Looks where he's pointing, blankly.*) Explain *what*?

TONY. (*Blinks, half-steps into closet, looks into depths, steps out again, a goofy smile on his face, but bewilderment, too.*) Uh—explain why there's no *film* in there!

IRVING. (*Agog.*) Is—is that *all* that's not in there? (*Rushes to door, peeks inside, turns with smile as goofy as* TONY's, *shuts door.*) You're right. Not a film in sight!

SAGAMORE. But why did you say it was a darkroom?

TONY. I was trying to impress Margo.

CORAL. How?

IRVING. (*Quickly.*) She always said he didn't know anything but greeting-cards! He wanted to show her how wrong she was.

SAGAMORE. Oh, that reminds me, Tony—Margo has said nothing but the nicest things about your skills as a poet!

CORAL. (*Incredulous.*) *This* Margo—?!

MARGO. (*Flustered.*) Well—Tony—you *are* awfully good at it, you know—despite everything.

TONY. But *Maggie*, even if that's *true*, you *know* I'd chuck it all for *you*! (*Winces as he realizes he's talking in couplets again;* MARGO *just sighs and shakes her head, but* SAGAMORE *chuckles.*)

MARGO. Sagamore, it wasn't that funny.

SAGAMORE. My darling, that was a chuckle of appreciation. It takes a real poetic genius to toss off rhymes so casually.

MARGO. That kind of talent is best appreciated from a respectful distance.

TONY. (*Absently hands mini-dress to* CORAL, *on:*) Like out of earshot?

MARGO. If the acoustics fit—!

IRVING. (*Quickly.*) Say, Sagamore, if you think *that* was good, you ought to take a look at his *professional* stuff—! (*Gestures in direction of desk, and* SAGAMORE *moves that way with interest, trailed by a less-than-enthused* MARGO.)

SAGAMORE. Yes, I'd like that!

MARGO. But really, Sagamore—!

SAGAMORE. (*Takes page from stack.*) Now-now, Margo, whatever your *personal* problems with Tony, you must admit he's got a real flair for poetry. (MARGO *sulks, and* TONY *beams with pride, as* SAGAMORE *reads:*) "Ere bills mount up, and babies cry, and your husband gives you a sock in the eye, I'd like to take this time to say—" (*Turns to flipside of page, reads:*) "Happy, Happy Wedding Day!" (MARGO *shuts her eyes,* SAGAMORE *belatedly reacts to what he's read and gingerly drops page back onto stack, with a nervous little laugh.*) Uh—maybe we *shouldn't* mix business with pleasure, after all.

CORAL. (*To save the sagging moment.*) Oh, Look! A record-player! Music is *so* nice at a party!

IRVING. (*Uneasily.*) Uh—Coral—

CORAL. (*Has already moved up to machine on table, sets dress there.*) Let's see what we've got— (*Slips stack from spindle, starts reading titles aloud, as* IRV *flashes a weakly apologetic smile at* TONY, *who starts to cringe as* MARGO *gives him a deadly stare, as they hear:*) "Remember" . . . "The Way We Were" . . . "Lover Come Back to Me" . . . "You're My Everything" . . . (*Belatedly realizes* IRV'S *not-so-subtle message, quickly sets recods down on table with a nervous smile, as:*)

MARGO. (*Speaks with venomous sweetness.*) "Put Them All Together, They Spell *Broth*er!" (*This last is inflected as if "Oh, Brother!", a put-down of what she imagines to be* TONY'S *ill-conceived attempt at subliminal hinting.*)

IRVING. Oh, who needs music!' Let's have fun! (*Shepherds* SAGAMORE *toward armchair-area.*) Sit down, have some snacks, I'll make us all some drinks!

MARGO. That's a marvelous idea! (CORAL *and* TONY *will each grab one of the dinette chairs, and bring them down to positions left of upstage armchair and between both armchairs, while* IRV *moves to liquor, and* SAGAMORE *sits in upstage armchair and* MARGO *in right armchair, and* TONY — *who has placed the between-armchairs chair — moves to get desk chair and roll it to position facing left, just below right armchair; all this occurs during dialogue:*)

SAGAMORE. (*Looking at plates of canapes.*) Say, those look good — what are they?

IRVING. Uh — why don't you *try* one and see if you can guess?

MARGO. (*Suspicious.*) Wait — you'd better let *me* try one, *first*, Sagamore — (TONY, *as dialogue continues, having placed desk-chair, kind of backs upstage from group, manages to sneak a glance at area behind screen, to take another surreptitious glance into closet, and even to peek quickly out into hall — always keeping a wary eye on group as he does so; he can't figure out what's become of* Lucille, *and it's driving him crazy.*)

Irving. (*Busily putting ice into five glasses.*) Hey, that's a good one, Margo!

Margo. What is?

Irving. Well, Sagamore *is* known as The Grunchies King — but who'd have thought he'd really have a *food-taster!*

Sagamore. (*Chuckles.*) Say, that *is* a good one!

Margo. (*Grimly.*) No it isn't. (*Grabs up canape from plate.*) Remember, you *are* on a restrictive diet, darling — I wouldn't want you to get sick!

Tony. (*This captures his attention — not unpleasantly, either — and he gravitates down toward group again, on:*) Restrictive diet? What a pity! What seems to be the trouble, old man? (Margo *reacts to last two words, but refrains from comment.*)

Sagamore. Well, you see, my *gerontologist* thinks that —

Margo. (*Quickly.*) Oh, *let's* not get into a *medical* discussion! Let's just have fun! (*Takes quick bite of canape, chews a second, goes wide-eyed, speaks queasily, her full-mouth words making her mumble.*) What *is* this stuff, anyhow!

Irving. (*Turns from liquor, hiding his glee, on:*) Why, it's your very favorite snack, Margo — melted marshmallow and Grunchies!

Sagamore. (*Elated.*) Grunchies? Margo, you never told me! We ought to put the recipe on the cereal-boxes!

Margo. (*Trapped, barely able to chew and totally unable to swallow, manages to mumble through a forged smile:*) Well — actually — they *might* not appeal to *everyone!*

SAGAMORE. Nonsense! Your taste has always been impeccable, Margo. If *you* like them, the whole *world* will like them!

IRVING. Excuse me, but what would everybody like to drink?

MARGO. (*Unable to keep all the desperation out of her voice.*) Anything! (*Then flashes a forced smile at* SAGAMORE, *and chews and chews with increasing unhappiness.*)

TONY. (*Sits down on chair between armchairs [*CORAL *has seated herself already on other dinette chair], on his line:*) She's marvelously easy to please.

SAGAMORE. Yes, she certainly is. Let's see — I guess I'll have a martini.

TONY. Sounds good to me.

CORAL. Me, too.

IRVING. Margo — ?

MARGO. (*Nodding vehemently while chewing away.*) Mrrrmph! (*Behind them,* LUCILLE *cautiously pokes her head out through archway, and over following dialogue will slip quickly up behind screen from right, then we will see her hand and arm reach out from begind screen and grab mini-dress from table, then pull it back behind screen; none of the others notice.*)

IRVING. (*Happily pouring gin and vermouth into glasses.*) If you want a change of pace, Margo, I have *cold* canapes in the refrigerator!

TONY. Oh, I didn't have a chance to put them into the bowls, yet. (*Starts to rise.*)

CORAL. (*Rises before he quite completes move.*) Oh, here, let *me* do it! A party-crasher should make herself useful.

TONY. Well, wait — you'll need a spoon — I think there's one in the cabinet.

CORAL. Oh, okay. Excuse me, Irving—(IRV *edges aside slightly, still continuing pouring drinks, as she opens cabinet, takes out saucer with pizza-wedge on it.*) What's *this* doing in there?

TONY. Oh, that's my dinner. I was so busy working, I never got around to it.

SAGAMORE. You keep it in a cabinet?

TONY. This apartment doesn't have a pantry.

SAGAMORE. But—cold pizza?

TONY. (*Shrugs.*) Bread, cheese and sausage—tastes just as good cold.

MARGO *has been valiantly chewing, still unable to swallow, but over last few lines her mood has switched from desperation to incredulity that everyone—including* SAGAMORE—*has been oblivious to her distress; when she speaks, she is getting both panicky and angry.*)

MARGO. (*Manages to say:*) "Mar-*hee*-hee—!"

CORAL. (*Has replaced pizza and located spoon in cabinet.*) *What* did she say—?

IRVING. Sounded like "mar-*hee*-hee?! (*Realizes.*) Oh! Her *martini*! (*Turns, grabs up one of the glasses.*)

TONY. (*Springs up, moves to get drink from* IRV, *on:*) Here, let *me*—! (*Brings it back to* MARGO, *who grabs it, drinks almost all of it in one grateful swallow, then gasps and goggles.*) A little strong, darling—?

IRVING. (*While* CORAL *heads upstage with spoon.*) It's *only* seven-to-one . . . ?!

SAGAMORE. (*Soothingly.*) Margo, you really shouldn't drink so *fast*!

MARGO. (*With a deadly smile toward* IRV.) But they're so *good* it's hard to *resist*!

IRVING. (*Quickly hands one to* SAGAMORE.) Here's yours!

SAGAMORE. (*Taking glass, raises it slightly.*) I'd like to

propose a toast to Tony's triumph!

TONY. (*Who has moved to cabinet and gotten drink of his own.*) I beg your pardon?

IRVING. (*Also taking drink from cabinet.*) Did you say "triumph"?

MARGO. Sagamore, what are you talking about?

SAGAMORE. (*Chuckles fondly.*) Well, you see, my dear—I have a little surprise for you *all.* . . .

CORAL. (*Has reached area left of range without looking at rear of screen, now turns on hearing his words, and reacts to what she sees behind screen:*) *Yipe*!

SAGAMORE. (*As* ALL *glance toward* CORAL.) What's the matter, my dear?

CORAL. (*Improvising desperately.*) The—the *refrigerator* is *cold*!

SAGAMORE. But—you're not *at* the refregerator— ?!

CORAL. Uh—I believe in planning ahead! (*Immediately steps out of sight toward refrigerator, and* MARGO *looks away, though the three* MEN *are still looking that way as* CORAL *opens refrigerator, and sharp silhouette of* LUCILLE— *writhingly trying to slip on that mini-dress—appears against translucent screen;* TONY *and* IRV *react with panic, and* SAGAMORE *with bewilderment.*)

SAGAMORE. She'd be a lot warmer if she left her *dress* on! (*CORAL closes refrigerator, and silhouette vanishes, as* MARGO *reacts to his words and looks upstage just too late to see what he's seen.*)

MARGO. If she *what*?!

TONY. (*Quickly.*) Hey, Sagamore, maybe you've had *enough*!

SAGAMORE. But I haven't even *tasted* my drink!

IRVING. Then maybe you'd better *not*!

SAGAMORE. Nonsense! I'm allowed *one* drink every evening. My doctor says it's good for me.

MARGO. (*Winces as* TONY *brightens.*) "All things in moderation"! That's what *Saint Paul* always said!

TONY. Even Minneapolis.

SAGAMORE. (*Laughs.*) Hey, that's a good one!

MARGO. (*Grimly.*) No it's not.

SAGAMORE. Margo, where's your party spirit?

MARGO. (*Relents.*) I guess I *am* being a grouch. I'm sorry. I'm just a little tense. You know — former husband — future husband — I *do* want everything to go well. . . .

SAGAMORE. And it's *going* to, my dear. Especially when you hear my surprise!

CORAL. (*Moving down to group with that tray, which now has bowls of something on it [NOTE:* CORAL *really doesn't have enough time to fill those bowls* IRV *brought earlier, so she should stash the empty bowls in the oven- part of the range, and a set of pre-filled bowls should be ready for her to put on the tray from inside the refrigerator]*) My, this is certainly an *evening* of sur- prises — ! (*Flicks unhappy look back toward screen.*)

MARGO. What do you mean?

IRVING. (*Quickly.*) This next canape! She's never seen anything like it!

SAGAMORE. How do you *know* that?

CORAL. (*Quickly.*) Irv just invented it *tonight*!

SAGAMORE. How do you know *that*?

CORAL. (*Now setting tray on coffeetable.*) Irving is *crazy* about keeping secrets!

IRVING. (*Quickly.*) I also minored in Espionage!

MARGO. (*Peering uneasily into one of the bowls.*) Irv — what in the world *is* this stuff?

IRVING. Let me put it this way — Margo, do you like ice cream?

MARGO. (*Nods.*) I do.

IRVING. Sagamore, do you like melted chocolate?

SAGAMORE. (*Nods.*) I do.

IRVING. (*Beaming.*) Good. I now pronounce you a hot fudge sundae! (*Whoops at his own joke, as does* SAGAMORE, *while* OTHERS *stare at him in disbelief.*)

SAGAMORE. Hey, that's *another* good one!

MARGO. (*Glumly.*) Well—as good as the *last* two! (*Then, again peering into bowl.*) But Irv—what is this stuff—*really*?

CORAL. Why don't you just taste it and see?

IRVING. It's one of your favorites!

TONY. I thought you just invented it?

IRVING. Yes, but Margo likes *anything* with *Grunchies* in it! (MARGO *reacts with dismay,* SAGAMORE *with elation.*)

MARGO. But—

SAGAMORE. (*Frowning.*) "But"—?!

MARGO. (*Quickly.*) But of *course* I do!

SAGAMORE. Then why aren't you eating it?

MARGO. I—I don't have a spoon!

IRVING. (*Whipping one out of cabinet.*) *Here* you are, my dear! (*Proceeds over to her, hands her a bowl and spoon.*) *Bon appetit*!

TONY. (*Stands, pulls* IRV *slightly out of earshot of group, between right armchair and desk.*) Irv, the whole idea of these canapes was to discomfit SAGAMORE, not to kill MARGO!

IRVING. (*Lays hand firmly on* TONY'S *shoulder, then says with a maniacal grin.*) If *you* can't have her, *no* one can! (*Gives soft, fiendish chuckle, rubbing his palms together, as* TONY *rolls eyes skyward in despair, and* IRV *turns back toward group, where* MARGO *is still hesitating over bowl, spoon poised, a feeble smile of anticipation on her face.*)

MARGO. Don't I—even get a *clue* what's in it?

IRVING. *Then* it wouldn't be a *surprise!*

SAGAMORE. *That's* true enough.

MARGO. (*Almost glares at him, but restrains herself.*) Well—here goes! (*Takes a spoonful; her eyes widen, she makes a slow attempt at chewing, and stops; she manages a smile, but—to anyone but* SAGAMORE—*she is obviously grinning through her nausea.*)

IRVING. (*Just as in a breakfast-cereal commercial:*) *Hey*—she *likes* it!

SAGAMORE. She certainly *seems* to! (*To* IRV.) *Now* will you tell us what it is?

IRVING. (*Beatifically.*) Grunchie Aspic!

CORAL. (*As* SAGAMORE *beams and* MARGO *gags, suggests with real sympathy.*) Margo, would you like to powder your nose—?

MARGO. *MMMRPH!* (*Rises quickly, leaving bowl and spoon on table, and she and* CORAL *both hasten off toward bathroom,* MARGO *well in the lead.*)

IRVING. (*Sits in chair left of* SAGAMORE, *and* TONY *in chair right of him, both leaning toward him with amiable smiles.*) That's quite a woman you've got there, Sagamore! (*Behind them all, unseen,* LUCILLE, *now in the mini-dress—which might have fit* CORAL, *but is far too short for her, barely concealing the lower part of her go-go-outfit—starts a careful tiptoe from behind the screen toward hall door.*) If she could only talk!

SAGAMORE. (*Smiles nostalgically, reminisces aloud:*) Margo. Margo. There's never been anyone like Margo. The most efficient secretary a corporate executive ever had. Practically runs the company for me. And—since we became engaged—she's forever at my side—smiling, caring, loving—she monitors every bite of food I eat—she makes certain I'm tucked snugly in bed by eleven o'clock every night—she counts every stair I climb — she's in constant contact with my gerontologist, so she can be sure to give me the right pills at the right time — with her beside me, I never miss taking my Geritol, my Vitamin E, my calcium pills — she is like a guardian angel to me — thanks to her, I always get the proper amount of rest, never over-exert myself, keep my body functioning like a well-lubricated machine, avoid cocktail parties, late-night reveling, smoking, overeating, any and all forms of decadence, debauchery or dissipation that could be hazardous to my health. (*Takes a sip of martini, sets glass on coffeetable, turns to* TONY — *then lunges and grasps* TONY's *two hands in his own, and says in a pitious croak of agony:*) You've got to take her back! (LUCILLE, *who had just taken hold of the knob of the hall door at this point, reacts, releases knob, stands there.*)

TONY. What — ?

IRVING. Do you mean — ?

SAGAMORE. It's been a nightmare, a nightmare! Her solicitude never stops! Her constant caring, caring, caring is driving me mad! (LUCILLE, *fascinated, now starts moving down toward group, unnoticed by them, and will end up standing just upstage of the area between* IRV *and* SAGAMORE, *during:*)

TONY. (*Not yet elated, just stunned into wide-eyed curiosity.*) But — Sagamore — it you feel that way — why did you propose to her?

SAGAMORE. (*Releases* TONY's *hands, sits up straight, staring out front, a haunted, hunted look on his face.*) I didn't. I mean, I did, but it was an accident, a horrible moment of bad timing — !

IRVING. I don't get it — how can you propose marriage by accident?!

SAGAMORE. (*A little more calmly, but still deep in*

misery.) It was a few days after her divorce — she hadn't mentioned it to anyone — pride, or something — and she'd just done a marvelous job on clinching a deal for a series of new Grunchie-manufacturing plants — and I said to her — I said to her —

TONY. (*Grips his arm sympathetically.*) Easy, fella, easy.

SAGAMORE. (*Swallows, smiles weakly.*) Thank you. I've got to get control of myself. (*Takes a breath, sighs it out.*) There. I'm all right, now. (TONY *releases him, and he continues, out front.*) I said, "Margo, you're a marvel. If you weren't already a happily married women, I'd propose to you right here and now!" (*Shudders, picks up martini, drains rest of drink.*)

IRVING. You don't have to say any more. We can imagine what happened next.

SAGAMORE. (*Hollowly, a doomed look on his face.*) And ever since that day — I've been searching, hoping, praying, for some loophole — some scheme — some insidious way to get your wife to return to you. It's my only chance!

TONY. Can't you just tell her you've changed your mind?

SAGAMORE. Margo? Impossible. She announced our engagement to the entire office. If I backed down, now, she'd slap me with a breach-of-promise suit that could take my entire company! I'm doomed. Doomed. Done for. Unless —

IRV AND TONY. Unless . . . ?

SAGAMORE. I have a plan. A desperate plan, but it's my only hope. That's the surprise I mentioned earlier. You see, from talking to Margo, I found out that your basic problem is one of economics —

IRVING. Not to mention talking in couplets!

SAGAMORE. Tony will have to handle that part, himself. I can only do so much. But money would be a nudge in the right direction.

LUCILLE. (*Caught up in* TONY's *and* IRV's *rapt attention to* SAGAMORE.) It sure would! (ALL THREE MEN, *startled, come to their feet.*)

TONY. Ye gods, what are *you* doing here?!

IRVING. You've got to get *out* of here!

TONY. Margo will be back any second!

LUCILLE. Tony, I *was* leaving, but then I remembered what a chilly night it is, and I can't find my topcoat anywhere—!

TONY. (*Waves a hand upstage frantically.*) It's behind the plant! Grab it and scram!

LUCILLE. (*Nods.*) Gotcha! (*To* SAGAMORE.) Awfully nice meeting you! (*Rushes upstage, starts getting coat from behind plant.*)

SAGAMORE. (*Still at sea.*) Who the hell is *that*—? (*Looks toward her, in her top-of-head-bow and dress that lets her legs show from hip to toe, and adds, uncertainly:*)—Shirley Temple?!

TONY. It's a long story, Sagamore—! (*Rushes up to* LUCILLE, *who, instead of slipping into the coat, is struggling out of the dress.*) What are you doing? You've got to get out of here!

LUCILLE. (*Almost out of dress, now.*) I just wanted to give you back your *dress*!

TONY. That's *Irving's* dress!

IRVING. *Keep* it! I've got *closets* full!

LUCILLE. (*Has dress off, now, and hands it to* TONY, *who grabs topcoat and holds it out to help her into it.*) You must tell me *more* about your friend sometime—!

CORAL. (*Appears in archway, stops in panic.*) Whoops!

TONY. (*Whirls, taking coat and dress with him.*) Ye gods, they're coming back!

LUCILLE. Oh, no! (*Ducks into closet, shuts door before a frantic* TONY *can hand her the dress or the coat.*)

TONY. Wait —! (*But it's too late.*) Oh, damn it —! (*Flings coat and dress behind plant, turns back toward archway just as* MARGO *appears there, and smiles feebly.*) Hi, honey! Back so soon?!

MARGO. I *will* be, if Coral will get out of my way —?!

CORAL. Oh. Sorry. (*Steps aside, and* MARGO *moves into room and down toward* SAGAMORE, *and* CORAL *shrugs helplessly at* TONY *and follows after her,* TONY *giving up and also moving that way.*)

SAGAMORE. (*Abruptly alarmed, looks at wristwatch, on:*) Hey, what *time* is it?!

TONY / IRV. (*Looking at their own wristwatches.*) Ten o'clock —!

SAGAMORE. (*Rushes to television set.*) *The Grunchies Hour* is coming on! (*Snaps on set, fiddles with channel-selector.*) We don't want to miss *that*!

MARGO. Oh, but really, Sagamore — must we? I mean, we're at a party, and it's very rude to —

SAGAMORE. Not in this case, darling! This is the big *surprise* I told you about! (*Over next few speeches,* ALL *will regain the seats they had earlier —* IRV *in desk chair,* MARGO *in right armchair,* TONY *on dinette chair between armchairs,* SAGAMORE *in upstage armchair, and* CORAL *on remaining dinette chair.*)

MARGO. Surprise? You mean — the surprise you had about *Tony*?

CORAL. What's that got to do with Grunchies?

SAGAMORE. You remember the jingle-contest we ran a few months back —? (TONY *is instantly way ahead of matters, and gets a look of terrified apprehension on his face.*)

MARGO. Oh! Of course! How could I have forgotten! They're announcing the *winner* tonight! . . . Tony, under the circumstances, I hope you don't mind if we watch? We'll turn it off as soon as we hear the winning jingle.

TONY. (*Who already knows what's coming.*) Uh—I *do* mind! Who ever heard of watching TV at a party! It's rude, Margo, rude—terribly gauche—it just isn't done!

MARGO. Well—if you really think—

SAGAMORE. Nonsense! Tony has a bigger stake in this thing than he knows!

MARGO. (*Starts to realize.*) Sagamore—what have you done?!

SAGAMORE. (*Still at TV, though* OTHERS *are now seated.*) Simply shown the respect I have for your integrity, my dear.

MARGO. (*Somehow sensing disaster in the air.*) *My* integrity—?

SAGAMORE. You've never *lied* to me, have you?

MARGO. Why—no, of course not!

SAGAMORE. And didn't you tell me that Tony was the greatest writer of snappy poems you'd ever known?

MARGO. Uh—yes—I guess I did—

TONY. (*Overcome.*) Maggie—sweetheart—you told him *that?*

MARGO. (*Angrily but almost tearily.*) Tony, you *are!* Whatever *else* you may be! And *don't* call me "*Maggie*"!

IRVING. Don't change the subject! I want to know what Sagamore did!

CORAL. Me, too!

SAGAMORE. I simply had the jingle-selection committee toss out *all* the other entries — and I had them accept Tony's — sight unseen!

CORAL. (*Elated.*) Tony! That winner gets *one hundred thousand dollars*!

IRVING. Hey! That's right! Tony — you're rich!

MARGO. (*Starting to share the panic she can see on* TONY'S *face.*) But Sagamore — sight unseen? Are you sure that was — uh — *wise*?

TONY. And it's so unfair to all the other contestants — !

SAGAMORE. Nonsense. The final decision would have been mine, even if I *had* read the other entries — but when I spotted Tony's name among the submissions, I *knew* what my move had to be! (*Glances at TV screen.*) Show's coming on! Quiet, everybody! (*Flips volume on, will go to his seat during:*)

ANNOUNCER'S VOICE. (*After FANFARE of trumpets from TV.*) Welcome to *The Grunchies Hour*! Ladies and gentlemen, as I'm sure you've already noticed, we did *not* begin the show with our usual musical theme — because — tonight we have a *new* theme! (*APPLAUSE comes from TV, and our* QUINTET — *eyes locked onto the TV screen similarly, though the emotional states vary:* SAGAMORE *fatherly and beaming,* IRV *and* CORAL *smilingly curious,* TONY *in bleak despair, and* MARGO *in apprehension — sits back and plays close heed to what follows.*) Yes, tonight we announce the winner of the Grunchies Jingle Contest, the winner of one hundred thousand dollars in cash, the creator of the jingle that was unanimously selected by our judges as the best melody, best lyric, and best description of the delights of *Grunchies*! (*More APPLAUSE.*) And the winner is — Mister Tony Dawson of Los Angeles, California! (*CHEERS and APPLAUSE.*) Congratulations, Tony! And now—here it is—the winning Grun-chies jungle, sung for you by the world-famous *Grun-chiettes*! (TONY *slides down a bit in his chair, shuts his eyes.*)

CHORUS. (*Sings:*)
THROW AWAY THAT SOGGY SANDWICH!
SEEK A CEREAL WITH PUNCH!
TOSS YOUR BROWN BAG IN THE BASKET
IF YOU'RE CRAVING FOR A CRUNCH!

WHY CHEW ON GOOEY TUNA IF
YOU'D REALLY RATHER MUNCH?

(TONY *has been sliding lower and lower, and* MARGO *is tensing and bracing herself for disaster, but* SAGAMORE *is by now smiling and rocking his head from side to side in thythm with the music, and* IRV *and* CORAL *smiling with pleasure, as the* CHORUS *finishes:*)
JUST GRAB A BOWL OF GRUNCHIES AND
YOU'LL WANT TO LOSE YOUR LUNCH!

(*Shouted:*) *Yeah*! (*On final words of song, before the shout, of course,* QUINTET *all react:* MARGO *and* TONY *cover their eyes,* SAGAMORE *comes to his feet, mouth agape in shock,* CORAL *goes wide-eyed and jams the knuckles of one fist into her mouth, and* IRV *leaps for the TV and manages to snap it off, on:*)

IRVING. Well, enough of that, let's get back to the par-ty—!

SAGAMORE. *I'm ruined*!

IRVING. Now, Sagamore—

SAGAMORE. (*To* MARGO.) *You're fired*! As my secretary *and* my fiancee! (*She bursts into tears—not plaintive, piteous tears, but a loud, sobbing "Waaaah!"*)

TONY. (*Stands.*) Wait, you can't blame *Margo*—!

SAGAMORE. (*Storming up toward closet.*) *Keep away from me, you maniac!* She *had* her choice—*my* kind of flake, or *you*! And she *blew* it!

IRVING. (*Hopefully.*) Does he still get the hundred thousand dollars? (SAGAMORE *stops, looks at him, gives an incoherent ROAR of rage at this demonstration of chutzpah, then yanks open closet door—and* LUCILLE, *in the go-go outfit, of course, steps out and hands him his topcoat, and* MARGO *sees her and gives an even louder "Waaaah!" as* SAGAMORE *strides to hall door, his coat in one hand, yanks it open, and storms out, on:*)

SAGAMORE. My board of *directors*— my *stockholders*— my *Grunchies*—! (*This last is a sob as he vanishes, not even shutting door behind him.*)

TONY. (*Rushes to door.*) Sagamore, wait—! (*Turns to* MARGO, *a picture of despair in the armchair.*) Maggie, honey, *please* don't cry! I'll just go *explain* to the guy! (*Then he winces, knowing he's done another couplet, and* IRV *shakes his head in despair, and* CORAL *slumps wearily in her chair, and* LUCILLE *turns and leans her forearm on closet-door frame and her forehead on the forearm, and* TONY *exits to hall, and* MARGO—*she does this the instant she hears that couplet, of course— gives a wall-shattering final "Waaaah!" as*—)

THE CURTAIN FALLS

ACT III

Half an hour later. Dinette chairs and desk chair are back where they belong. All canapes and containers have been cleared. Folding screen is folded and leaning against right wall below refrigerator. Papers are gone from desk and typewriter. Closet and hall doors are closed. Liquor items are still atop cabinet.

At curtain-rise, CORAL *is found seated in upstage armchair, holding a martini, and* MARGO *in right armchair, also holding a martini. When they speak, it will at once become obvious that* MARGO *is at least two martinis ahead of* CORAL, *but her semi-slurred speech and maudlin mood will be left up to the actress playing the role, and only indicated when necessary; caution should be taken, however, that however slurred her words may be delivered, they should all be understandable.*

MARGO. (*Takes sip of her drink, then:*) How long does it take to die of cirrhosis?

CORAL. When you get there I'll let you know. (*Sips her own drink.*)

MARGO. (*Sips.*) What am I going to *do*?

CORAL. (*Sips.*) What *can* you do?

MARGO. (*Sips.*) I can keep *drinking*.

CORAL. (*Sips.*) Then *that's* what you're going to do. (MARGO *sniffles and stifles a sob.*) What's the *matter*?

MARGO. What *isn't* the matter?

CORAL. I mean specifically.

MARGO. (*Drains drink, sets it on coffeetable, counts*

76

on fingers.) Lemme see . . . I don't have a job—

CORAL. Check.

MARGO. I don't have a husband—past *or* future . . .

CORAL. Check.

MARGO. I don't have a house or car . . .

CORAL. (*Blinks.*) You don't?

MARGO. I gave them all to Tony.

CORAL. You gave them *both* to Tony.

MARGO. That's what I *said*.

CORAL. You said all.

MARGO. All what?

CORAL. House and car.

MARGO. What about them?

CORAL. You gave them to Tony.

MARGO. (*Nods.*) So did I! (*Wobbles to her feet, gets empty glass, heads for bar, and will pour a straight gin with no ice, during:*)

CORAL. Margo—?

MARGO. "Maggie."

CORAL. But you *hate* that name.

MARGO. That's all right. Right now, I hate *myself.*

CORAL. Oh. (*Sips her drink, then:*) Maggie—?

MARGO. I hate that name.

CORAL. Margo—?

MARGO. That, too.

CORAL. I've got to call you *something.*

MARGO. (*Turns with drink, but leans back against cabinet for support.*) Why?

CORAL. Because I want to ask you a question.

MARGO. What question?

CORAL. "Why?"

MARGO. Why *what*?

CORAL. Why did you give your house and car to Tony?

MARGO. (*Straightens, frowns, reels back to armchair.*) I forget. (*Sits with a plop.*)

CORAL. There must have been a reason.

MARGO. For what?

CORAL. Giving the house and car to Tony.

MARGO. Oh, *that*! (*Sips.*)

CORAL. Yeah, that. (*Sips.*)

(*Until otherwise indicated, each will precede her speech with a sip of her drink, during:*)

MARGO. Because Tony didn't have a house or car.

CORAL. That was very generous.

MARGO. It was stupid.

CORAL. Why?

MARGO. Because now *I* don't have a house or car. Or husband. Or job.

CORAL. You could have.

MARGO. How?

CORAL. Go back to Tony.

MARGO. I can't.

CORAL. Why not?

MARGO. (*Does not drink, sets glass on coffeetable.*) He doesn't love me.

CORAL. (*Does not drink, sets glass on coffeetable.*) Then why does he want you back?

MARGO. Because he *thinks* he loves me.

CORAL. And *you* don't?

MARGO. *Love* me?

CORAL. Think *he* does.

MARGO. No.

CORAL. Why not?

MARGO. Because of his job.

CORAL. Writing greeting-cards?

MARGO. Right!

CORAL. What's that got to do with loving you?

MARGO. Everything.

CORAL. I don't get it.

MARGO. It's very simple . . . (*Speaks with great care, over-enunciating words.*) Tony writes greeting cards — because — the world is full of little people —

CORAL. (*Nods.*) Like at Munchkinland.

MARGO. (*Hasn't even heard her; continues carefully:*) — little people who don't know how to com-mu-ni-cate . . .

CORAL. So?

MARGO. So Tony *helps* them.

CORAL. *That's* nice of him.

MARGO. *No* it's not.

CORAL. *Why* not?

MARGO. (*Her noice degenerating into a sob.*) *I'm* a little person — why doesn't Tony ever help *meeeee* — ?! (*This last is a wail of self-pity that ends with her face buried in both her hands.*)

CORAL. That's what he's doing right *now*!

MARGO. (*Uncovers face.*) He is?

CORAL. He ran after Sagamore, didn't he? He's going to plead with him, isn't he? He wouldn't do that if he didn't love you, would he?

MARGO. (*Shrugs.*) *You* tell *me*!

CORAL. Maggo, I just did. Those were — rhetorical — questions.

MARGO. "Maggo"?

CORAL. (*Frowns, tries again.*) Marggy.

MARGO. No. That's not right either.

CORAL. (*Shrugs.*) Then you must be — an imposter. (*Picks up her glass, heads for liquor.*)

MARGO. Well — what about the go-go girl in his closet?

CORAL. (*Pouring a straight gin, no ice.*) That was

Lucille. She's only a copy editor.

MARGO. Dressed like that?

CORAL. Irving's dress didn't fit her.

MARGO. Then she should give it back. (*Picks up her glass from table.*)

CORAL. (*Returning with drink to plop into armchair again.*) That's what she's doing!

MARGO. She is?

CORAL. (*Sips; then, patiently:*) Irving took her down to his apartment to shop in his closet, remember?

MARGO. No. (*Drains her drink.*)

CORAL. Sure you do. *Right* after Tony left. Right after *Sagamore* left.

MARGO. Which?

CORAL. Both. Sagamore left, Tony left. Then Lucille and Irving left.

MARGO. (*Waves a hand vaguely deskward.*) Then where is Tony's greeting-card copy?

CORAL. Lucille took it with her, to read.

MARGO. In Irving's closet?

CORAL. I guess. (*Drains about half her new drink.*)

MARGO. (*Sets her empty glass on coffeetable.*) I hope she's got a strong light. (*Giggles.*) And a stronger stomach.

CORAL. *That's* the spirit! (*Drains rest of her drink.*)

MARGO. *What* is?

CORAL. (*Considers; then shrugs and amiably repeats the pronoun:*) *That!* (*Sets empty glass on coffeetable.*)

MARGO. (*Considers; then:*) Oh. (*Then* BOTH *look up as hall door opens and* TONY *storms in, slams door, then just stands there glaring at them.*)

TONY. I hope you're *happy*, Maggie!

CORAL. (*Sagely.*) See? He cares.

MARGO. Oh, thank you, Tony.

TONY. (*Loses a fraction of pent-up anger, switches to surprise.*) Are you *smashed* . . . ?

MARGO. No. But I am working on it. Busy-busy-busy-busy—

TONY. (*Takes a step nearer, stops.*) Maggie—you *are* smashed!

MARGO. That's prediculous! . . . I mean—riposterous!

CORAL. (*To* TONY.) She means "ridicterous" . . . (*Frowns, looks ceilingward, asks herself aloud:*) "Prepostulous"?

MARGO. (*Waves both hands vaguely.*) Whatever!

CORAL. Oh! Tony—? Did you catch up with Sagamore?

TONY. (*His rage returning.*) *No*! And do you know *why* I didn't?! . . . I got *arrested*!

MARGO. (*Slightly sobered.*) What?!

CORAL. What for?!

TONY. (*Raging in frustration.*) *Attempted mugging*!

CORAL. Mugging *who*?

MARGO. *Sagamore*?

TONY. Ha! No such luck! I never got anywhere *near* him! (BOTH WOMEN *have managed to get to their feet, now, and move up to him as he explains, boiling with frustration:*) See, he drove off in his limousine just as I got downstairs, so I started to run after him—I figured he'd have to stop for a red light, or something—except there was this lady in my way, and when she saw me coming, *she* started to run!

CORAL. She thought you were *after* her?

MARGO. Oh, Tony!

TONY. The next thing I knew, there was this *cop*, running after *me*, and shouting for me to halt or he'd *shoot*! So I stopped, and I tried to explain that I was *chasing* a car!

CORAL. And?

TONY. He thought I was *nuts* — tried to offer me a nice *dog biscuit*!

MARGO. But why didn't you *explain*?

TONY. (*Wearied by the memory.*) Oh, I *did*, I *did*! It wasn't easy — by now, a crowd had gathered, and the woman was still screaming, and I started getting afraid they were going to *lynch* me — !

CORAL. So what did you *say*?

TONY. I explained that I was chasing the car because my wife's *fiance* was in it, and I was trying to bring him *back* to her!

MARGO. Oh, great! They must have *really* thought you were nuts, *then*!

TONY. No, as a matter of fact, they didn't. There were a lot of *married* men in the crowd, and they said they knew *just* how I felt.

MARGO. But what about *Sagamore*?!

TONY. Hell, by the time I *convinced* everyone I wasn't a *lunatic*, he was *long* gone!

CORAL. Then — the cop let you *go*?

TONY. Not exactly. I got a *ticket* — for *Malicious Jaywalking*!

MARGO. Awww!

CORAL. Poor Tony!

TONY. Oh, hell, I don't want to talk about it any more! (*Gloomily moves to liquor, pours himself a drink, during:*) I'm sorry, Maggie, really sorry — I did my best!

MARGO. Oh, I know you did, Tony, and I really appreci—(*Stops, eyes widening queasily, a hand to her stomach.*) *Oh*-oh! (*Speaks carefully.*) I think—think I'm going to—

TONY. Ye gods, not in *here*!

CORAL. (*Grabs her, steers her toward archway.*) Quick, into the bathroom!

MARGO. (*A hand over her mouth by now.*) Mrrrmph! (TONY, *drink in hand, takes a few steps after them as they vanish through archway, but stops as door opens and* IRV *and* LUCILLE *come in—she is now wearing another mini-dress, but its length is more suited to her height, except that the color is a sickening gray-and-green-striped material.*)

IRVING. (*Rushes to him, leaving* LUCILLE *to close door.*) Tony, we've saved your marriage! Margo is *yours* again!

TONY. (*With a glance toward archway.*) If she *survives*!

LUCILLE. Tony, he's serious! We figured the whole thing out!

TONY. *What* whole thing?! What are you talking about?!

IRVING. California Law!

LUCILLE. It was one of Irv's minors!

TONY. (*Scornfully.*) What *wasn't*! (*Takes large swallow from his drink.*)

IRVING. (*Hurt.*) Well, if you *don't* want to *hear* my discovery—!

TONY. Oh, sure, sure, why not! Go ahead—what idiot scheme have you cooked up now?!

LUCILLE. It's *not* an idiot scheme—it's actual California Marriage Law!

TONY. There's a distinction?

IRVING. (*Exasperated.*) Look, Tony—a divorce is a public trial—and a madman isn't competent to stand trial!

TONY. Thank you, Clarence Darrow! But what's that got to do with *me*?

LUCILLE. Tony, Tony—where do you keep your supper?!

TONY. On a plate in the cabinet.

IRVING. And where do you sleep?!

TONY. (*Gesturing.*) On those armchairs—You *know* that!

LUCILLE. On *both* of them?

TONY. (*Impatient.*) I face them toward each other across the coffeetable—it makes a fairly comfortable bed—if I don't roll over.

IRVING. And what do you use your alarm clock for?!

TONY. To remind me to stop *work*, of course. (*Reacts to their beaming smiles.*) Oh, come *on*, now—I know it sounds a little *eccentric*, but—

LUCILLE. But what about all the *other* things?!

TONY. (*Uneasily.*) *What* other things? (LUCILLE *and* IRV *will duplicate ticking items off on their fingers as each speaks in turn over next five lines:*)

IRVING. Hiding a singer from Munchkinland in your shower!

LUCILLE. Keeping a go-go-girl in your closet!

IRVING. Pretending your closet is a darkroom!

LUCILLE. Talking in couplets!

IRVING. Washing your dishes in the shower!

TONY. (*Who has been brightening with each new addition.*) Hey, and don't forget the *dog biscuits*!

LUCILLE. *What* dog biscuits?

TONY. A cop offered me some when he arrested me for chasing a car!

IRVING. (*Clutches* LUCILLE *nervously as they both*

take a backsetp.) Hey, maybe he really *is* crazy!

TONY. It could have happened to *anyone*! (*When they still look dubious:*) Well—*almost* anyone. . . .

IRVING. (*Relaxing enough to at least release* LUCILLE.) Okay, okay, we can *use* it—and there must be *dozens* of other things you do that we don't even *know* about—!

TONY. Hold it! Look, let's say I *could* convince a court I was nuts, and they *did* dump the divorce decree—what *good* would it do me? I'd wind up in the *loony bin*!

LUCILLE. But just *think*—when you got *out*—Margo would be *waiting* for you!

TONY. Yeah, with a *baseball bat*! (*Drains rest of drink, takes glass back to cabinet.*)

CORAL. (*Appears in archway, looking worried.*) Tony—is there some place Margo could lie down?

TONY. (*Leaves glass, starts toward her.*) She's still sick—?

CORAL. Well—actually—I think she's over the *worst* of it—if you know what I mean—but she's really in lousy shape to drive home. . . .

LUCILLE. (*Turns on* IRV.) You and your Grunchie-snacks!

TONY. No, no, it wasn't that—at least, not entirely—! (*Is looking toward armchair area and scowling.*) She could have *my* bed—and I could sleep on the floor—except—she'd *probably* be better off on the *floor*!

IRVING. Listen, she could always use *my* bed!

CORAL. Then where would *you* sleep?

IRVING. (*Shrugs.*) My bed. (*When they all stare.*) It's a king-size.

LUCILLE. But Irv—you—and Margo—in the same bed?

IRVING. Hell, any wife of Tony's is a wife of—(*Sees*

TONY'S *look, stops.*)

CORAL. (*Has moved down to join group by now.*) Well, wait — I have *twin* beds at *my* place — and my roommate's out of town —

IRVING. I accept!

CORAL. For me and *Margo*, I meant!

TONY. But how would you *get* her there?

CORAL. (*With less assurance.*) Well — you and Irv could carry her downstairs to the sidewalk, and I could flag a cab —

TONY. (*Holds up a forestalling hand.*) And if that *cop's* still out front, he'll think I'm working with a *gang* of woman-snatchers!

LUCILLE. We could *explain* —

IRVING. How do you explain to a speeding *bullet*?!

LUCILLE. Okay, how about we fix up Tony's armchair-bed for *Margo*, and then *Tony* could sleep with Irv?!

TONY. Irv didn't pay his water bill. What if I had to brush my teeth during the night?

CORAL. Brush them before you go.

TONY. I mean, had to brush them *real bad*?! (MARGO *enters, much sobered but very queasy, and slowly makes her way down to group, unnoticed by any of them.*)

IRVING. (*Exasperated.*) Hell, why don't we just stand here *arguing* all night, and by then the problem will be *over*!

LUCILLE. Be serious, Irving — Tony's got to find *someplace* to put Margo to bed!

MARGO. *What*? Now *just* a *min*ute — ! (ALL *react to her unexpected interruption.*)

TONY. Margo!

IRVING. I thought you called her "Maggie" — ?

TONY. When she's this mad, I can't take chances.

CORAL. Margo, I just thought you were too sick to drive.

MARGO. (*Mollifed.*) Oh. But I'm not driving—I'm taking a cab.

TONY. What did you do with my *car*?!

MARGO. *Your* car?!

TONY. You gave it *back* to me, remember?!

MARGO. Surely you're not going to *hold* me to that?!

TONY. Boy, you're a great one for weaseling out of promises!

MARGO. When did I ever weasel *before*?!

TONY. What about your *marriage* vows?!

MARGO. Oh. Those. Well . . .

LUCILLE. Why don't you two fight in the morning? You'll be fresher then.

MARGO. And miles apart, if *I* can help it!

CORAL. Oh, come on, you're all wrung out. You've got to stay *here*!

MARGO. Here?! I'd *die* first!

IRVING. Then it's settled. Go sleep in *my* bed, Margo. Tony and I will make other arrangements.

MARGO. (*A hand to her stomach.*) Maybe I'd better. I'm really afraid I'd better lie down someplace, and soon, or—

LUCILLE. (*Takes her arm.*) Here, I'll help you get there.

MARGO. (*Uneasily.*) Then I'd better not look at that *dress*!

LUCILLE. What's *wrong* with my dress?

MARGO. It reminds me too much of a *Grunchies* box!

LUCILLE. You know, I *thought* these colors looked familiar!

IRVING. Where do you think I got my inspiration when I *made* it?!

TONY. Irv! *You* eat *Grunchies*?!

IRVING. *Somebody's* got to do it!

MARGO. (*At door with* LUCILLE *by now.*) Not me. Never again. Not as long as I live . . . If I do. (*They exit.*)

IRVING. That poor kid! No husband, no fiance, no job, no house, no car—

TONY. Oh, I'm not *really* keeping the house and car. That was just my broken heart talking.

IRVING. Then I'm glad you *didn't* decide to bunk with me. Some broken hearts talk all night.

TONY. Irv, even if you *had* paid your water bill, I wouldn't stay there. What if we died in our sleep? You've got a closetfull of *dresses*!

IRVING. (*Hurt.*) To-ny!

TONY. Oh, hell, nothing personal, buddy—there are just some places I'd rather not be found dead. How could I *explain* to people?!

CORAL. (*Put a protective arm across* IRV's *shoulders.*) Tony, stop it! Only a really *macho* man would have the *nerve* to take up dressmaking *and* the track team!

IRVING. (*Stunned with delight.*) Coral! You care!

CORAL. (*Quickly removes her arm from him.*) Well, wait—I don't really—I mean—well, maybe a little—but even so, Irv—*twenty thousand* a *year* and you can't pay your *water bill*?!

IRVING. I didn't say I *couldn't* pay it—I just *didn't*! Anyone can forget! What kind of spendthrift do you think I am?!

CORAL. Well—

IRVING. (*Hopefully.*) You know, with *forty* thousand a year, we wouldn't even *need* water—we could shower in *champagne*! (LUCILLE *re-enters from hall, alone.*)

LUCILLE. Coral, there's something you should know—!

IRVING. Not *now*, Lucille, I'm on a *roll*!

LUCILLE. Well, hold the dice, Irving, this is important! Coral, while Margo was getting ready for
bed—(*Breaks thought to comment to* IRV.) You really
carry a lovely selection of nightgowns! (*Returns to topic
with* CORAL.)—I tried to phone Munchkinland to get a
message to my girl friends I was supposed to meet
there—

TONY. But who'd be inside to answer the phone?

LUCILLE. Some guy named Shorty.

CORAL. *Shorty* crossed that musclebound *picket-
line*?!

IRVING. Maybe he tiptoed *under* it.

LUCILLE. You don't understand. The strike is *over*!

TONY. So soon? That must be the fastest strike on
record!

CORAL. Did Shorty *settle* with the big guys, or *what*?

LUCILLE. He didn't *have* to! See, all these hunks were
pacing back and forth in front of the club, when all the
girls in go-go-outfits started showing up for the contest—and—well—

IRVING. They decided there were better things in life
than picketing?

LUCILLE. You got it, Buster! They all paired off and
went their merry ways, and Shorty got the joint open
right on schedule.

CORAL. (*A gasp of dismay.*) Oh, no! I never showed
up for work! And Shorty said if I missed one more time
I was through! And my rent is due on Monday!

IRVING. (*Fondly.*) Forty thousand dollars pays a lot
of rent—

CORAL. (*Sighs.*) All my life I've searched for a man
who'd be kind, gentle, thoughtful, tender—(*Shrugs.*)
But what the hell! (*Goes into impassioned clinch-kiss
with* IRV.)

TONY. Coral—do you know what you're *doing*—?!

CORAL. (*Stops kissing long enough to shrug and say:*) Getting a great education! (*Resumes kissing.*)

LUCILLE. (*Peers closely at the pair.*) From the look of it, so is Irving!

TONY. (*Resigned.*) Well, at least I don't have to write her new act, now.

IRVING. (*Breaks from kissing.*) Don't count on it—I think I can get her a booking at the Union Building! (*Starts to resume kissing, but then* ALL *react as there comes a KNOCK at the door, and* IRV *and* CORAL *disembrace.*)

LUCILLE. *Who* can that be at *this* hour?

IRVING. Maybe *Margo* has to brush her teeth!

TONY. Hey, yeah, you're right! The poor kid—! (*Starts for door.*)

CORAL. Be careful—it could be a policeman with dog biscuits.

IRVING. (*Who, of course, hasn't heard the arrest-story.*) And if it *is*?

CORAL. We may have to buy Tony a leash. (*Then* TONY *opens door, and* ALL *react as* SAGAMORE *steps in.*)

QUARTET. (*In unison.*) *Sagamore*!

SAGAMORE. I have decided to be forgiving.

TONY. (*Coolly.*) Do we all turn handsprings, or just fall down and kiss your feet?

SAGAMORE. (*Uncomfortably.*) Now, Tony—

TONY. *Mister* Dawson to you, Bub!

LUCILLE. Breaking poor Margo's heart!

CORAL. Just because Tony wrecked your company!

IRVING. (*Huffily.*) And you never even *touched* my canapes!

SAGAMORE. (*Resignedly.*) In other words—if anyone should apologize, *I* should? Very well. I apologize.

TONY. I'll pass your remorse on to Margo. (*Starts to shut door.*)

SAGAMORE. (*Moves into room a bit further, quickly.*) Well, wait, I'm not finished.

IRVING. If *he's* gonna turn a handspring, *I'm* leaving the *room*!

SAGAMORE. Please, will you all hear me out—?!

LUCILLE. Before we *throw* you out?

CORAL. Oh—let him have his say. I mean, the poor man *is* out of *business*!

IRVING. Maybe you could get him a job at Munchkinland—of course, he'd have to scrunch down a little.

TONY. (*Controls himself, shuts door, folds arms, faces SAGAMORE.*) Okay, let's hear it. Then, if you don't mind, we have *important* matters to discuss!

SAGAMORE. (*Quite subdued, and sincerely contrite.*) Very well. When I left here, I did not go home, but directly to my office, to find out how much damage had been done our company image by Tony's jingle. The switchboard was lighted up like a theater marquee—call after call after call, from viewers who were still watching the show.

CORAL. Still watching? *That's* a good sign . . .

SAGAMORE. But they were threatening to turn it off, unless—

TONY. Unless what?

SAGAMORE. Unless we *repeated* the jingle!

OTHERS. *What*?!

SAGAMORE. (*Flings his arms overhead and shrugs, totally baffled.*) It's the first time that's happened in the history of the show. Of any show, for all I know!

IRVING. (*To TONY.*) Now you've got *him* talking in couplets!

LUCILLE. But—that means—they *liked* it—!

CORAL. Or couldn't believe their ears the *first* time!

SAGAMORE. Oh, they liked it, all right. Thought it was marvelous the way we kidded the product. From the consensus of those calls—if one can trust a statistical sampling—what with even people who had *never* eaten Grunchies about to switch over—sales should *triple*! Do you know—we played that jingle over *five times*—and by the time the show went off the air, callers were *still* begging for more?!

TONY. Talk about gluttons for punishment!

IRVING. Do you mean listening to the jingle or eating the Grunchies?!

TONY. Both!

SAGAMORE. (*Takes a check out of his topcoat pocket.*) Tony—I believe I owe you one hundred thousand dollars.

TONY. I hope you don't expect an argument! (*Grabs check, and while he's happily pocketing it:*)

LUCILLE. Under the circumstances—I take back what I said about throwing you out.

SAGAMORE. And Tony—there's one other thing . . .

IRVING. Careful, Tony—it may be a year's supply of Grunchies!

SAGAMORE. Heavens, I'd never do *that* to him! I want to stay on his *good* side!

TONY. You do? Why?

SAGAMORE. Because I want to sign you to an exclusive contract to write all future jingles for my company. (*As* TONY *and* OTHERS *react with pleased shock:*) In case it hasn't occurred to you—by tomorrow, every sponsor in television will be trying to do the same, Tony. I thought I'd get *my* bid in first.

IRVING. Which *is*—?

SAGAMORE. A hundred thousand a year. To start.

CORAL. Oh, Tony!

LUCILLE. Take it, quick!

IRVING. Please, Tony, please—I always wanted a rich friend!

SAGAMORE. Tony—what do you say?

TONY. (*Finally finds his breath to say:*) Hell, for a hundred thousand a year, I'll even *eat* the damned stuff! (*Reaches out and shakes* SAGAMORE'S *hand.*)

SAGAMORE. And as a special bonus—I'll—I'll even take back Margo.

TONY. What?! But Sagamore—!

SAGAMORE. No, no, don't thank me. I owe you that much. Our marriage will work out. Somehow. (*Looks so miserable,* OTHERS *roar with laughter.*) What's so funny?

TONY. Sagamore—I *love* Margo! When you broke off your engagement, you made me the happiest man in the world!

SAGAMORE. (*The dawn of hope.*) You mean—you'll take her *back*—you really *mean* it—you *want* her back?!

TONY. Of course I do!

SAGAMORE. Good heavens, man—*WHY*?!

TONY. (*From the heart.*) Because she is the sweetest—the nicest—the gentlest—the kindest—(*Hall door opens, and* MARGO *lurches in, one hand on her stomach, her face ghastly, the other hand flailing at arm's length at* IRV, *toward whom she moves on tottering steps, clutching her nightgown about her.*)

MARGO. *Irving* . . . You *birdbrain* . . . why didn't you *tell* me you have a *waterbed*?! (*Then her eyes widen, a hand goes to her mouth, she shifts direction and exits, fast, toward the bathroom.*)

CORAL. (*After a moment, as* OTHERS *still look toward where* MARGO *was.*) Tony must have the busiest bathroom in Los Angeles!

IRVING. (*Takes her arm.*) She can't stay in there forever. Come on back to my place—we can start going over your curriculum!

TONY. Sagamore—I just remembered—Margo's job . . .

SAGAMORE. She's got it back. With a hefty raise. But I'll leave *you* to tell her about it when she recovers.

LUCILLE. Yeah, I'd better be going, too. You and Margo will have a lot to talk about.

SAGAMORE. Can I give you a lift?

LUCILLE. Are you talking about my spirits, or this weary old frame?

SAGAMORE. (*Looks more closely at her.*) Both, if you like. Do you have any plans for the evening?

LUCILLE. Nothing that I can't abandon with pleasure. But—why this sudden interest, Sagamore?

SAGAMORE. Well—I always *was* a sucker for Shirley Temple! . . . But—even more than that—it's the oddest thing, but—when I look at you—for some reason, I think of Grunchies!

LUCILLE. (*Reacts—with pleasure, since from* him *this is a* compliment—*then looks down at her dress, and quickly away from it, on:*) What a *lovely* thing to say! Though I can't imagine *why*?! (LUCILLE *and* SAGAMORE *exit, arm in arm.*)

IRVING. (*Shakes* TONY'S *hand.*) Well—I wouldn't have believed it earlier today, buddy—but your future has taken a definite turn for the better!

CORAL. (*Takes* IRV'S *arm.*) Hey, what about *mine*?!

IRVING. (*Releases* TONY'S *hand, takes her in his arms.*) When you've got me—you've got everything! (*Kisses her, then starts leading her toward door.*) It's gonna be so great — you and me — alone together every night — there's so much to learn!

CORAL. Are the courses very hard?

IRVING. Who's talking about *school*?! (*They exit;* TONY *closes hall door, glances bathroomward, then rushes to liquor and pours a pair of drinks; just as he finishes, a rather wrung-out* MARGO *enters via archway, comes to end of platform upstage of rail, sees him, and stops.*)

MARGO. Where did everybody *go*? Didn't I see *Sagamore* back here when I was passing through?

TONY. It's a long story, Maggie. Come on over to the nice comfortable chair, sit on my lap, and I'll tell you all about it.

MARGO. (*Takes a step, then stops.*) Wait a minute — is that extra drink for *me*? Because if it *is* — ! (*A hand goes to her stomach.*)

TONY. No, they're both mine. With the condition you're in — I have a lot of catching up to do.

MARGO. (*Moves toward him, hesitantly.*) Oh, Tony — what are we going to do? I've lost my job — my fiance — and I won't take back the house or car, no matter what you say —

TONY. Don't you mean what are *you* going to do? None of those things affects *me* . . .

MARGO. (*Moves a little nearer.*) No, they *all* happened to me — but — don't you even *care*?

TONY. (*Steps down to desk, sets drinks there, turns to her.*) Well — I suppose if I *still* cared for you a *little* —

MARGO. (*Miserable.*) A *little* — ?

TONY. Well, it's hard to care for somebody who thinks your life-work is a lot of garbage . . .

MARGO. Oh, but I don't — not really — I never did — you're tops at what you do, Tony — you always were — it was just the stupid *money* — but now — with me out of a job — *you* make more than *I* do — so — well —

TONY. Maggie — even if I made a hundred thousand a year — I'd *still* be talking in couplets! (*Sits in upstage armchair.*)

MARGO. (*Moves down beside armchair.*) If a woman loves a man — really loves him — I guess she can get used to anything —

TONY. What woman are we talking about?

MARGO. Oh, honey — (*Sits on arm of his chair.*) I could *try* — really try — to get used to it —

TONY. (*As if trying to reach a decision.*) You honestly *would*?

MARGO. (*Hesitates; then:*) If I honestly *could* . . . ! (*He reacts, smiles at her, then tests her again.*)

TONY. Even without *riches* — ?

MARGO. (*Starting to smile.*) You bet your *britches*! (*Slides gently down onto his lap, slips her arms about his neck, as his arms go about her waist.*)

TONY. You'd *never* leave me, *never*?

MARGO. I'd stick it out *forever*!

TONY. (*With a wicked gleam in his eye.*) Till our hair had turned to *silver* — ?!

MARGO. (*Opens her mouth, starts a nod, then stops in chagrin.*) Aw, Tony! That's not fair!

TONY. Shut your mouth.

MARGO. Why?

TONY. As I mentioned a few minutes ago — I have a *lot* of catching up to do! (*Kisses her firmly, fondly and finally fiercely, and she is kissing back with equal fervor, as —*)

THE CURTAIN FALLS

"GRUNCHIES JINGLE"

Throw a- way that soggy sandwich! Seek a cer-e-al with punch! Toss your brown bag in the basket if you're craving for a cranch! Why chew on gooey tuna if you'd really rather manch? Just grab a bowl of Grunchies and you'll want to lose your lunch! Yeah!

LIST OF PROPERTIES

ACT I

Preset:
Page in typewriter
Bottle of whiskey in deepdrawer of desk
Glasses in cabinet
Icecubes in refrigerator

Tony:
Must wear beach-thongs, no sox

Irv:
Coral's dress when he follows her out of bathroom

ACT II

Clear:
Used glasses from cabinet
Whiskey bottle from desktop

Preset:
Liquor, ice bucket, glasses on tray, atop cabinet
Close window drapes
Stack of completed verses next to typewriter
Page in typewriter
Pizza slice on saucer in cabinet
Spoons in cabinet
Pre-filled bowls of aspic in refrigerator

Irv:
Phonograph, records, stacked bowls for first entrance
Wristwatch
Tray of canapes for second entrance

TONY:
Wristwatch

CORAL:
Mini-dress over arm for entrance

MARGO:
Mini-dress over arm for re-entrance

SAGAMORE:
Wristwatch

ACT III

CLEAR:
Canapes, tray, papers from desk, used glasses

PRESET:
Screen folded against right wall below refrigerator
Dinette and desk chairs back where they belong
Both doors closed
Drapes still closed
Martinis for CORAL and MARGO on coffeetable ready for
    top of act

SAGAMORE:
Check in pocket of topcoat

LUCILLE:
New mini-dress with gray-and-green stripes [NOTE:
she'll need to take her topcoat when she exits with
SAGAMORE, so have her enter carrying it over her arm,
and leave it someplace handy for her exit]

SOUND EFFECTS:
Telephone bell

Alarm clock bell
Pre-taped television program

SPECIAL INSTRUCTIONS:
1. Have a floodlight in refrigerator (the audience never sees refrigerator when door is open) for the silhouette-effects; regular refrigerator-light would be of insufficient brightness onstage;
2. Have LUCILLE use escape at left end of closet for her trek to area outside right archway, so that blackout can be brief, rather than having her actually cross stage in darkness;
3. Height of coffeetable should be same as armchair-seats, or a little lower, to make feasible TONY's claim to sleep across these three items; and
4. Naturally, your cast-members are the ones who pre-tape ANNOUNCER and CHORUS for the "Grunchies Hour" sequence.
CURTAIN CALL:
Stage is bare, doors shut. Then Lucille peeks out of closet to right, then left, then "sees" audience, smiles, comes DL for bow. Then Sagamore enters from behind screen, eating bowl of cereal, "sees" audience, reacts, leaves bowl on table, comes DR for bow. Then Coral races on from "bathroom" with Irving in pursuit, crouches facing him left of upstage armchair; both "see" audience, react, he gestures her to take first bow, and she comes down beside Sagamore and does so, then he comes down beside Lucille and bows. Then Margo rushes in from "hall," hand on mouth as if about to upchuck, stops above right armchair as she "sees" audience, reacts, then comes down center to bow, then moves beside Irving as Tony rushes in from closet extending Lucille's coat (as in Act Two), "sees" audience, reacts, drapes coat over back of left armchair, comes down center and bows. Then rest of cast moves to hand-in-hand stance with Tony, all bow, and curtain falls.

- Stage Setting -
"YOUR FLAKE OR MINE?"

Sky Backdrop

Picture Window

Drapes

Walk-In Closet

(escape)

Hallway

(escape)

plant

Cabinet

Range

Refrigerator

chair

Dinette Table

chair

Armchair

Coffeetable

Armchair

Tv Console

Folding Screen
[8" platform]

Railing

Bulletin Board

Swivel Chair

Desk with
Typewriter
& Telephone

Bathroom

Proscenium

Proscenium

MUSIC USE NOTE

Licensees are solely responsible for obtaining formal written permission from copyright owners to use copyrighted music in the performance of this play and are strongly cautioned to do so. If no such permission is obtained by the licensee, then the licensee must use only original music that the licensee owns and controls. Licensees are solely responsible and liable for all music clearances and shall indemnify the copyright owners of the play(s) and their licensing agent, Samuel French, against any costs, expenses, losses and liabilities arising from the use of music by licensees. Please contact the appropriate music licensing authority in your territory for the rights to any incidental music.

IMPORTANT BILLING AND CREDIT REQUIREMENTS

If you have obtained performance rights to this title, please refer to your licensing agreement for important billing and credit requirements.

www.ingramcontent.com/pod-product-compliance
Lightning Source LLC
Chambersburg PA
CBHW070342120726
47909CB00008B/2720